KANADA

KANADA

EVA WISEMAN

Tundra Books

Copyright © 2006 by Eva Wiseman

Published in Canada by Tundra Books,
75 Sherbourne Street, Toronto, Ontario M5A 2P9

Published in the United States by Tundra Books of Northern New York,
P.O. Box 1030, Plattsburgh, New York 12901

Library of Congress Control Number: 2005910619

Library and Archives Canada Cataloguing in Publication

Wiseman, Eva
    Kanada / Eva Wiseman.

ISBN-13: 978-0-88776-729-6
ISBN-10: 0-88776-729-X

1. Holocaust, Jewish (1939–1945) – Juvenile fiction.   2. Auschwitz
(Concentration camp) – Juvenile fiction.   3. Refugees – Hungary –
Juvenile fiction.   4. Refugees – Canada – Juvenile fiction.   I. Title.

PS8595.I814K35 2006   jC813'.54   C2005-907302-0

We acknowledge the financial support of the Government of Canada
through the Book Publishing Industry Development Program (BPIDP)
and that of the Government of Ontario through the Ontario Media
Development Corporation's Ontario Book Initiative. We further
acknowledge the support of the Canada Council for the Arts and
the Ontario Arts Council for our publishing program.

ONTARIO ARTS COUNCIL
CONSEIL DES ARTS DE L'ONTARIO

Typeset in Goudy

Printed and bound in Canada

This book is printed on acid-free paper that is 100% recycled,
ancient-forest friendly (40% post-consumer recycled).

1 2 3 4 5 6   11 10 09 08 07 06

For my parents,
who lived the horror and emerged triumphant

"We shall draw from the heart of suffering itself
the means of inspiration and survival."
— Sir Winston Churchill

Europe: June 1944

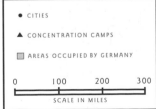

CITIES

CONCENTRATION CAMPS

AREAS OCCUPIED BY GERMANY

0   100   200   300

SCALE IN MILES

Europe: End of May 1945 – August 1946

*Although Austria was already divided up by the Western Allies, the city of Vienna was further subdivided into five zones. The Americans, Soviets, French, and British were each in charge of one zone. The control of the International Zone, in Vienna's Inner City, alternated every month among each of the powers.

I

Limbo

Sunday, February 13, 1944

"Why aren't you ready? Tamas is waiting for us at Castle Hill!" said Klari. She stood in the doorway of my house bundled up in a heavy coat, letting in a gust of cold air before shutting the door.

"I was just putting on my boots," I replied. "But why are you here? Weren't we supposed to meet at your place?" I had been getting ready to call on Miri Schwarz, my second best friend, who lived across the street. The two of us had planned to pick up Klari and spend the afternoon tobogganing with her and her brother.

"You're right. It's just that my father doesn't want . . . I mean . . . I was afraid he would . . ." Klari was flustered.

"What are you talking about?"

She didn't answer. She looked uncomfortable. "Who cares about Father's nonsense? Everything is just fine," she said. "Let's get Miri. Put on your warmest jacket. It's freezing."

She seemed so miserable that I let the matter drop, but I filed it away in a corner of my mind.

As we crossed the street, we waved to Mr. Kristof next door, shoveling the snow from the sidewalk in front of his house.

"Where are you girls off to?" he called after us.

"We're going tobogganing!"

"Have fun! It's a perfect day for it," he said, waving good-bye.

Miri was waiting for us at her front door, her slight figure wrapped in so many layers of clothing that she looked as wide as she was tall.

"Where is your sled?" she asked in greeting. "Should I bring mine?"

"No need," said Klari. "Tamas took ours to Castle Hill."

We trudged through the snowy streets, past Papa's grocery store. Mama had surprised us by running it with great success ever since Papa and my brother, Dezso, had been conscripted. Down the street, I checked to see what was playing in the cinema that Miri's parents owned. We crossed the town square, which boasted three ornate churches. Every Sunday morning, Klari and her family attended the one with the tallest spire, while Miri and I went to Jewish school at the synagogue. Finally, we arrived at the edge of town and Castle Hill.

The steep incline, rising sharply against the cloudy sky, was covered with a soft white powder. The laughter of tobogganers and skiers intermingled with the sound of the church bells ringing in the cold, pure air. Tamas, tall, blond, and handsome, was at the foot of the hill, stomping his feet to keep warm. By the time we all pulled our toboggan to the top of the hill, we were panting. I kicked a piece of ice over the crest. It rolled and rolled down the long slope. The bottom seemed very far away. The sled was long, so there was room for all of us on it.

"I want to sit in the middle," said Miri.

"I'll be at the rear, behind her," said Klari.

Tamas laughed, flapping his elbows up and down. "Cluck, cluck, cluck! Both of you are big chickens! Are you a chicken too, Jutka? Do you want me to sit at the front?"

"Hi, Jutka!" I looked over to see Agi, an older girl, trudging toward us. She waved a cheery hello. Jonah Goldberg was pulling her toboggan. Agi was two grades ahead of me in school, in Tamas's class. Jonah had graduated last June.

"Agi! Jonah?" said Tamas.

"I have a few days leave from my regiment," explained Jonah.

"What are you waiting for?" said Agi. "The hill looks a lot steeper than it really is."

They jumped on their sled and flew down the hill before I could ask Jonah anything about Papa and my brother.

"See, Jutka? There is no need to be afraid," Tamas reassured me.

I leaned over the edge of the hill. "It's a long way down!"

Tamas hopped onto the sled. "I'll be the navigator! Come on behind me! It's perfectly safe." I didn't want to seem like a coward, so I squeezed in behind him and wrapped my arms around his waist, with Miri and Klari sliding in behind me.

"You're a good sport, Jutka," said Tamas.

I couldn't tell whether the quick beating of my heart was due to the warmth of his body against mine or the thought of swooshing down such a steep hill at breakneck speed.

My stomach lurched as we whizzed through the powdery snow, but by our third turn we were all laughing. We plodded up the slope and slid down again and again until all of us were out of breath. Finally, Miri threw herself onto the snow.

"I am so tired!" she groaned. "Do you remember how we used to make snow angels when we were kids?"

She spread her arms and legs and swept them through the snow. Soon all of us were lying on the frosty hill, and the white blanket surrounding us was etched with angels. I was making my best figure when a soft snowball disintegrated on the tip of my nose. I shot up and caught Tamas patting another handful of snow into a ball.

"I'll get you for that!" I packed a scoop of snow tightly between my palms, just like Dezso had taught me. "I'll get the rest of you too!"

Klari and Miri retaliated against my attack, and in no time all of us were dusted in white.

*

A few benches dotted the snowy field around Castle Hill. We sat down on one of them for a rest.

"I am going to get you girls chestnuts," Tamas announced.

He bought two packets of roasted chestnuts wrapped in newspaper from a vendor by the side of the road. He handed a bag to Klari. "That's for you and Miri," he said. "Jutka and I will share this one."

Klari giggled and jabbed her elbow into Miri's side. I shot them a murderous glance.

We sat on the bench, munching on the chestnuts. They warmed my frozen fingers and heated my insides. I couldn't think of anything to say that would impress Tamas, so I sat quietly. When Tamas smiled at me, I knew that my silence didn't matter.

2

Saturday, March 18, 1944 –
Sunday, March 19, 1944

"Checkmate!" Dezso's voice rang triumphant as he confiscated my queen.

"What do you mean? How did you . . . ?" I suddenly realized that I had left my queen defenseless.

"Jutka, how many times do I have to tell you that you must always defend your queen?"

I grinned at him. It was incredibly wonderful to have him and Papa home.

Dezso was irritated because I didn't pay attention. He took his chess seriously, and we spent many hours at the chessboard. I was a good player, but he was much better.

"Let's have another game," he said. "I want to see if you have completely forgotten everything I taught you. It's too easy to beat you!"

I stuck out my tongue and tried to focus on the chess-board, but I couldn't. The warmth of the March sun streaming through the window, the memory of the rich potato soup we had eaten for lunch, and even the sight of Dezso's disconsolate face made me contented and drowsy. When the doorbell rang I was startled back to wakefulness. Dezso and I stared at each other for a long moment. My heart hammered.

"Are you expecting somebody?" he finally asked.

"No . . . and Mama and Papa didn't say anything about a visitor either." Our parents had left the house an hour ago to visit Grandmama.

The bell rang again.

"Don't answer! Maybe they'll go away," Dezso said. As if on cue, the doorbell pealed again.

"I think I should get it, in case . . ." I didn't have to finish my sentence. Dezso understood.

It could be anybody, I told myself as I hurried to the front hall. It might be Klari or Miri. *Please, God*, I prayed silently, *don't let it be a gendarme with orders for Papa and Dezso to leave us immediately — or even worse!*

My heart stopped pounding when I saw the mailman's friendly face. He was holding a large box wrapped in brown paper and tied with twine.

My voice came out in a squeak. "What have you got for us, Mr. Horvath?"

"A package from Canada."

"Canada? Who do we know in Canada?"

"Well, missy, you must ask your parents that, not me," he chuckled.

Dezso examined the wrapping carefully. Papa's name, ARMIN WELTNER, was printed on it in bold capital letters, as was our address. CANADA was written in the top left corner, but the name of the sender and the address were missing. Dezso shook the parcel.

"Easy does it!" I cautioned. "It might contain something breakable! Who could have sent this to us? Do we know anybody in Canada?"

"I think Papa has a cousin in Canada. This parcel must be from her. I wonder what's in it?"

"Let's open it and then we'll know!"

"Don't be a snoop. It's not addressed to you." He put the box down on a chair and turned back to the chessboard. "Now, pay attention, or I won't play with you again."

He trounced me in two more matches before we heard the key turn in the front door. Papa was carrying two large suitcases. Mama was behind him, carrying Grandmama's wooden stool. Grandmama followed them into the room. When we showed Papa the package, he raised his hand.

"Whoa!" he said. "The package can wait. We must get Grandmama settled first. It's too difficult for her to manage without Karolina." Grandmama's housekeeper had had to leave her when it became illegal for Christians to work in Jewish households.

"We'll take care of you, Grandmama!" I hugged her as hard as I could. She smoothed my hair.

"You're a sweet child," she said, "but it isn't easy to leave your own home."

Papa helped Grandmama to an armchair. Dezso placed the wooden stool in front of her.

"Rest your legs for a while," he said.

"Shall I get you something to drink?" Mama asked her.

"I am fine, dear." Grandmama closed her eyes, her face ashen.

"We must get hold of your medicine somehow, even if it means the black market," said Papa.

Grandmama's eyes flew open. "Don't worry about me! I am just fine!" She forced a smile. "This is very exciting. Open the package!"

Mama got a knife from the kitchen and cut the twine. Papa undid the layer of wrapping and found a letter.

"It's from my cousin, Iren," he said. "She lives in Ottawa." The name meant nothing to me.

"The capital of Canada," Papa explained.

"How are we related to her?" I asked.

"Iren's father and my father were cousins," said Papa. "Her father left for Canada when I was a boy."

He began to read. "Iren sent us this parcel because she was worried that there would be food shortages because of the war."

Mama laughed ruefully. "That's one way to describe it. I wonder if people in Canada realize how bad things are

11

here. I'll write her and ask her to send us Grandmama's heart medicine!"

"It's worth a try, but don't count on it," said Papa. "It's a miracle that this package even got to us."

There were bags of flour and sugar, tins of sardines and beans and Spam, cans of coffee, and colorful boxes of crackers and cookies. There was even a small wooden crate filled with oranges. At the bottom of the box lay a slim, rectangular book. On its cover was a picture of two men on horseback. They were dressed in crimson jackets and wore wide-brimmed hats, their figures set against an endless blue sky and snowy mountains. The book's title was simply *Canada*.

Mama leafed through it. "It seems to be about Canada," she said. "I wish that I could read English."

I reached for the book. There were a lot of illustrations and photographs. I saw pictures of Indian chiefs with feathered headdresses fighting soldiers in uniforms. There were cowboys on horseback and pictures of covered wagons driven by people in old-fashioned clothes. Most of the photographs were of churches, of streets full of cars and well-dressed people, and an official-looking building. There were mountains and fields of wheat. A picture of the Arctic snow, so vast and so white, looked more pure and clean than anything I'd ever seen.

"When the war is over, I'll go to Canada and see these places," I told Mama. "I'll take Dezso with me."

She ruffled my hair. "Perhaps Papa and I will come with

you too." She sighed happily. "The book's lovely, but this food will go a long way."

"We're lucky," said Grandmama. "The customs officials at the border must have missed it."

"Armin, it was so nice of your cousin to think of us," said Mama.

Papa did not reply. He was gripping the pages of the letter so tightly that his knuckles had turned white.

"What's wrong?" asked Mama.

"Too late! Too late!" he muttered.

He crumpled up the letter and pitched it hard into the corner of the room. The ferocious expression on his face frightened me. "Iren says she wants to sponsor us to come to Canada," he said. "It's too late now! Too late!"

Papa had tried to get us documents that would allow us to leave Hungary. He had lined up for days in front of the Canadian consulate in Budapest only to have his application turned down. The United States also rejected us. They didn't want Jewish immigrants.

"Does Iren say why she didn't reply to any of our letters?" asked Mama.

"She didn't get them, not a single one," said Papa. "She says that she became worried when she didn't hear from us." He slammed his fist into his palm in frustration. "And now it's too late!"

"Calm down, Armin," said Mama. "We only have you and Dezso home for one more day. Let's not spoil it. At least dinner tonight will be really good."

*

As I lay in my bed, I told myself that Mama was right. Supper had been delicious. The Spam was a little salty, but I hadn't had meat in so long that I didn't mind. I had almost forgotten how good strong coffee tasted. Best of all were the oranges – juicy and sweet. Mama saved the rinds to make candied orange peels with the sugar Iren had sent us. I ate so much that I felt I would burst. For the first time in a long time, I went to bed with a full stomach.

The sound of distant thunder woke me. The clock on my bedside table showed that it was ten o'clock in the morning. I pulled the blanket over my head, determined to fall asleep again. It was Sunday, but Mama had let me skip Jewish school because Papa and Dezso were home. The blanket was ripped off my face. Dezso was standing over me, his expression grim.

"Get up! Quick!" he cried. "The Germans are here!"

What we dreaded the most had happened.

I jumped out of bed and threw on my clothes. A few moments later, we were standing at the back of a crowd lining the broad expanse of Kossuth Street. It seemed as if the entire town had turned out to welcome the German army with flowers and loud cheers. Dezso and I looked at each other in sorrow. It was hard to hear his quiet "Let's go home" over the happy roar of the crowd.

Papa and Dezso left for the forced labor regiment that afternoon. Mama and I went with them to the railway station. It was too far for Grandmama to walk, so she had said her good-byes at home. The railway station was humming with activity. Jonah Goldberg and his parents were farther down the platform. Agi was with them. Jonah had one arm around Agi, the other around his mother. Uniforms were everywhere. A group of Arrow Cross men glared at us. German soldiers stood laughing, rifles slung over their shoulders. A gendarme in a tall, plumed hat came over to us.

"Let me see your papers," he said to Papa.

Papa handed over his documents, the word *Israelite* stamped across them. The gendarme scowled.

"Where do you think you're going, dirty Jew?" he asked.

Dezso's face burned crimson. "Don't talk to my father that way!"

The gendarme's hand moved toward the revolver holstered at his waist.

Papa squeezed Dezso's arm, and my brother fell silent.

"My son and I are returning to our labor regiment on the Austrian border," Papa said mildly. "I am sorry, sir. My son is young and foolish. He doesn't realize what he is saying." He turned to Dezso. "Son, apologize to the officer immediately!"

"I won't!"

"Apologize, son!"

Dezso glared at Papa. Papa glared back. Dezso was the first to lower his eyes.

"I'm sorry," Dezso said, as if the words were being torn from his throat. I breathed easier when the gendarme's hand moved away from his pistol.

"Let me see your papers, boy." He checked Dezso's documents carefully.

"Your papers seem to be in order," he said. He sounded disappointed. "You better learn to mind your tongue!"

Dezso cracked his knuckles, a sure sign that he was angry. The gendarme handed back Dezso's papers.

"You Jews have two minutes to get out of here. When that train leaves, you better be on it!" He strode away.

Papa turned to Dezso. "How dare you jeopardize your own life and the lives of your mother and sister with your foolish tongue! Can't you get it through your head that they have guns and we do not. And now that the Germans are here . . . you must use your brain, my son, in order to stay alive. We must be patient. The war will be over soon."

"We've been patient for too long, Papa," muttered Dezso.

"You've heard the same rumors I have – the Germans are losing the war on all fronts." Papa laid his hand on Dezso's shoulder. "Remember, son, as long as we don't challenge them, we will survive. It's our only chance."

"You must be more careful," said Mama. "I beg you to be more careful!"

Dezso hugged her.

"I promise, Mama," he said.

As we said good-bye, Papa wiped away my tears.

"We'll be home before you know it," he reassured us. "Be a good girl, Jutka. Help your mama and grandmama. Be strong."

I forced a wobbly smile.

The train whistle blew. The cold, gritty air made my eyes water. Papa and Dezso climbed the metal steps leading into a passenger car. They pressed their faces against a window and waved to us. Mama and I waved back until our arms hurt and their faces became too small to see.

3

Monday, April 3, 1944 — Wednesday, April 5, 1944

I unbuttoned my jacket in the warm spring air and peered down the street. There were no German or Arrow Cross uniforms in sight. It was almost eight o'clock. Miss Szabo was livid when we were late for school. The bell pealed while I was dashing up the worn staircase. The heavy doors banged shut behind me, and I paused to catch my breath. The scarred wooden floor, the walls paneled in cherrywood, and the old-fashioned light fixtures had a comforting familiarity. The pungent smell of chalk mixed with sweat and the odor of gym shoes made me feel at home.

My classroom door was wide open. Chatter and laughter drifted into the hall. I was in luck! Miss Szabo had not yet arrived. I sat down at the desk I shared with Klari at the front of the room. Miri sat behind us.

Half of the period had passed by the time Miss Szabo finally came into the room. She was closely followed by Principal Nemeth, dressed in his Arrow Cross uniform and tall, shiny boots. Miss Szabo's cheeks were flushed and her considerable bosom was heaving. She plucked at her lace collar.

"Attention, students! Principal Nemeth wishes to speak to you."

Nemeth puffed out his chest. He stood for a long moment, twirling one of the shiny buttons of his uniform.

"I have an important announcement to make!" He paused for dramatic effect. "From now on, all Jews must sit at the back of the classroom!"

Everyone was silent, except for Miri, who gasped with a ragged, painful sound. She and I were the only Jewish students in our class. I stared at Nemeth dumbly. Then, with a will of its own, my arm shot up.

"Excuse me, sir," I said before being given permission to speak. "I don't understand!"

Nemeth tugged on his mustache. "You heard me. All Jewish students must sit in the back row against the wall!"

I forced myself to speak again. "Why?"

The principal took a step toward me and bent over my desk, so close that I could see the blackheads peppering his nose. He looked at me with so much venom that I felt paralyzed.

"Why?! Why?! You dare to ask! I'll tell you why! Because I say so!"

He stepped back and clapped his hands. "Attention! All Jews attending the fifth form, pick up your belongings and move over there!" he bellowed, pointing to an empty desk by the back wall. As Miri and I gathered up our books, Miss Szabo stood by the principal's side, silent, her eyes fixed on the floor, her hands clasped. Klari helped me move my things. Her face was so pale that her freckles stood out like ink spots.

"I am sorry, Jutka. I am so sorry," she mumbled.

The others stared at us. Maria Kovacs began to giggle. She was hushed by the girl sitting next to her.

When Miri and I settled into the empty desk by the wall, she grasped my hand under the table.

"This is unbelievable," she whispered. "What can we do?"

"I don't know if we can do anything. He is the principal."

"Quiet!" Nemeth roared. He gave a satisfied nod. "Make sure you stay there!" He cocked his finger at us. "I'll be coming back regularly to check on you!"

Miss Szabo stood at the front of the room, her eyes still fixed on the floor, not speaking. When the classroom door banged shut behind Nemeth, she looked up.

"Try to forget about this unfortunate incident," she finally said in a hoarse voice. She glanced at the clock ticking on the wall. "We still have some time. Let's make the most of it. We'll pick up our geography lesson where we left off yesterday."

She unrolled a large map and tacked it to the wall. With a long pointer, she indicated the different continents. She located Hungary. Next, her stick moved to the west, to Germany. She traced Germany's borders with the pointer.

"This is an old map, out of date," she explained. "It shows what our world looked like a few months ago. Things have changed since then." She unrolled another map and tacked it up beside the first one. "As you can see, the borders of Germany have expanded under the leadership of Adolf Hitler. The shaded areas of the map are countries that have been occupied by Germany." Following the movement of her pointer, we could see that Germany had taken over not only our own country but also much of Europe. Next, Miss Szabo pointed to the map of North America. All of Europe could have fit into a corner of Canada or the United States.

The bell rang, and we began to gather up our books.

"One more minute, please," said Miss Szabo. "As you know, every year students in my class participate in a writing contest. The winner this year will receive a framed certificate with his or her name on it. I will also display the winning entry on the wall for all of you to read. I want each one of you to choose a country you would like to live in. Explain the reasons for your choice in five or six pages. Even if you pick Hungary, you must explain the reasons for your choice. Any questions?"

General groans, but no hands were raised.

She smiled broadly. "Come on, you might even enjoy this assignment. I want you to hand it in two weeks from today. If there are no further questions, class is dismissed!"

Klari made her way to our desk.

"Nemeth is out of his mind! I'll come over to your house later, Jutka, to do our homework, but I've got to run now. I have a math test next period."

Nobody else came near us.

Miri and I were the last to leave the room. As we passed her desk, Miss Szabo stopped us.

"I am very sorry for the humiliation you girls endured today," she said, "but I have to go along with Principal Nemeth. I am on my own. I need my job to put food on the table. Can you understand?"

"Did they really make a law about where school kids are supposed to sit?"

"Listen and listen carefully. What I am going to tell you must stay between us," she said. "There is no such law, but you must do as Principal Nemeth says. He is an ignorant man, but he is very powerful in the Arrow Cross. And you know what that means."

We did. Members of the Arrow Cross party hated all Jews passionately.

The next morning, Mama appeared at the door of my room. She was wearing a blue dress with a small cloche perched on her head.

"Time to get up!" She pulled open the drapes. I peered at the alarm clock by my bedside and burrowed deeper into my pillows.

"Give me ten more minutes." I had gone to bed late. Mama, Grandmama, and I had spent hours discussing

Principal Nemeth's orders. By the time we resigned ourselves to the fact that there was nothing we could do about it, it was midnight.

"Get dressed!" said Mama. "You must leave for school early because I am coming with you. I am going to have a word with Nemeth."

I threw back the covers. "You can't, Mama! We agreed last night that I have to do as he says!"

"I couldn't sleep a wink," said Mama. "I won't be able to live with myself if I don't speak to him."

"You can't do that, Mama! You'll get me in trouble!"

"Don't be childish, Jutka," she snapped. "He is not fair. The law is on our side. We'll go to the police if we have to. Get dressed!"

Mrs. Gombos, the gorgon guarding Principal Nemeth's door, stared at us coldly.

"What can I do for you, Mrs. Weltner?" she asked.

"Good morning, Mrs. Gombos," said Mama. "We'd like to see Principal Nemeth."

"The principal gave me express orders that he did not want to be disturbed."

Mama drew herself up and said calmly, "We will not be leaving until we have seen him."

The secretary snorted. She stomped into the principal's office. As she closed the door behind her, I had a glance of Nemeth in his chair, bent over a pile of papers on his desk.

Mrs. Gombos reappeared. "The principal refuses to see you."

Mama grabbed my hand and pulled me toward Nemeth's door.

"You can't go in there!"

"Try to stop me!" Mama swung open the door. I was close on her heels.

Nemeth glanced up, his pen suspended in midair.

"Have you lost your mind, woman?" he roared.

"I am sorry, Principal, but we had to see you," said Mama quietly. "My daughter told me that you ordered her and her friend to sit at the back of the class. We were hoping that you would change your mind and allow Jutka and Miri to move back to their regular seats."

"How dare you question my authority!" He sprayed spittle.

Mama did not flinch or retreat. She raised her hands and wiped her face.

"We're not questioning your authority, Principal," she said with immense dignity, "but please allow me to point out to you that there are no laws in Hungary that support your decision." I only knew how upset Mama was by the damp patches her palms left against the light-blue material of her dress.

"I make the rules in my school! No Jew will tell me what to do," Nemeth added, showering Mama's face again.

"Very well," Mama said and turned to me. "Come, Jutka, we must inform the police of Principal Nemeth's actions." When I swung the door open, I almost knocked over Mrs. Gombos.

"Go to the police, if you like!" Nemeth cried. "A lot of good it will do you! The police chief is my cousin."

Mama was so angry that she could barely talk as we made our way to the police headquarters.

"Take it easy, Mama. I really don't care where I sit." That wasn't true, but I wanted her to calm down. It broke my heart when I had to move to the back of the room, but I wished that I had never told Mama about it.

"The law is on our side," she said.

The police station was a squat gray building at the end of Rakoczy Street. We climbed the worn steps. A large poster was taped to the heavy front door. Mama was about to enter, but I pulled on her arm.

"Let's read the notice first."

The poster said:

ATTENTION ALL JEWISH RESIDENTS
OF PÁPA!
AS OF APRIL 5, 1944, EVERY JEWISH
PERSON SIX YEARS OF AGE OR OLDER
MUST WEAR A TEN-CENTIMETER SIX-
POINTED CANARY YELLOW STAR ON
HIS/HER GARMENTS. THE STAR MAY BE
MADE OF CLOTH OR SILK OR VELVET. IT
MUST BE PROPERLY SECURED TO THE
LEFT SIDE OF CLOTHING. ANY JEWS
CAUGHT NOT WEARING THIS BADGE
WILL BE IMMEDIATELY INTERNED.

No matter how many times we read the notice, the words did not change. From the next day onward, we would not be allowed to leave our homes without wearing a yellow star setting us apart.

"I don't believe it," Mama said. "It's sad, so sad."

I grabbed her hand. "Believe it! It's here in black and white. Surely you can see now that going to the police is stupid. If they make us wear a yellow star, they won't care if Nemeth makes us sit in the last row or on the roof."

"You're right. If they are willing to do this" – Mama pointed to the notice – "then it would be useless to complain. I'm so sorry, darling." She hugged me.

"Let's go home, Mama. Let's get out of here while we still can."

"Where are we going to get the yellow material to make these stars? I don't wear yellow. It makes me look sallow."

"The skirt Grandmama sewed for my birthday is the right shade of yellow."

"Darling, no! Not your new skirt!"

"Grandmama can make me another skirt when the war is over. If I show up at school without a star, Nemeth will punish me for sure."

I need not have worried. Early the next morning, a knock on the front door woke us up. It was Miri. She had come to tell us that new posters had appeared overnight on the town walls. Jewish students were no longer allowed to go to school.

*

Mama, Grandmama, and I sat around the kitchen table, coffee and toast untouched.

"You must keep up with your schoolwork," said Grandmama. "Klari will tell you what to read in your textbooks."

Mama reached for her coffee cup and set it down again without drinking. "I'll help you."

"I don't need help. I can do it by myself."

"Fine, as long as you don't get behind."

Grandmama stood up. "If neither of you wants breakfast, let's clear the table."

Mama and I helped her wash the dishes. When we were done, Grandmama dried her hands.

"Go get your yellow skirt, Jutka," she said.

The skirt was in my closet. I took it off the hanger and buried my face in the crisp material. I had planned to wear it in the summer. I went back to the kitchen and Grandmama pulled me close.

"Don't worry . . . I'll make you an even nicer skirt when the war is over. I promise."

"I know you will. It's just that it's so pretty . . . Let me help you cut out the stars."

"I'll help too," Mama said.

"Why don't you both help by bringing me the clothes you want me to put stars on," said Grandmama.

We piled up sweaters, jackets, and dresses beside the sewing machine. Mama even took out Papa's and Dezso's clothes so Grandmama could get them ready for their next visit home. When we were done, Mama sat down at the

27

piano. The plaintive notes she coaxed from the ivory keys seemed full of fear.

I wandered around my room aimlessly. It felt strange not being at school. The lace curtains cast dappled shadows across my things. I walked over to the bookshelves above my desk and picked up a straw doll. I straightened her skirt. Next to her on the shelf was a music box Mama had given me for my birthday. I cranked its handle and a Mozart lullaby filled the room. The Canada book was on the top shelf. I picked it up and started leafing through it. I looked at the pictures of Indians in tall headdresses, cowboys on horseback, and people in old-fashioned clothes driving covered wagons. I was most interested in the pictures at the back of the book: the photographs of tall buildings, streets full of cars and masses of people. As far as I could see, there wasn't a single uniform in sight, nor was anybody wearing a six-pointed star. Although the people in the photographs seemed to be in a rush, many of them were smiling, despite the falling snow. It looked clean and orderly and peaceful – so peaceful.

I stood in front of the window, staring out at the empty street. I decided to do my assignment for Miss Szabo's writing contest. I knew that if I gave it to Klari, she would take it to school for me and ask Miss Szabo to mark it. Who knows? I might even win the prize.

I sat down at my desk, opened up my notebook, dipped my pen into a bottle of ink, and began to write. The words flowed from my pen so rapidly that I didn't have time to stop and think. It was as if the words had been stored in my soul and were pouring out of me onto the paper. I wrote about how I wished with all my heart that I lived in Canada, because it was a country where nobody had to wear a yellow star; where fathers and brothers did not have to leave their families for forced labor regiments; where girls like me could go to school; where I would meet Indian chiefs with colorful headdresses; where the streets were paved with gold (although I had to admit that I wasn't sure if this was true).

When I finished my composition, I could barely keep my eyes open. The feather comforter and pillows on my bed looked so inviting that I stretched out on top of them and closed my eyes. The neighing of a horse startled me. I was no longer lying in my bed but in the back seat of a beautiful sleigh pulled by two white horses galloping across a field of pure white snow. The snow was so blinding that I could not see where the blue sky began and where the white field ended. I was shivering despite the rays of bright sun high in the sky, so I pulled the hood of my parka over my head. Mama was sitting next to me. She took my hand.

"You look so pretty with the fur framing your face," she said.

"She certainly does," said Grandmama from my other side.

Papa and Dezso were in the front seat. Papa held the reins. Dezso turned around. "Do you want to go faster?"

I nodded. Papa pulled in the reins, and the horses began to gallop at top speed.

"Look!" Mama cried. A figure on horseback was silhouetted against the field of snow. "There is a cowboy on his horse!" As we passed, the horse reared up and the cowboy tipped his hat.

"There is somebody else behind them!" Dezso said. "It's an Indian chief!" The man's tall headdress displayed the colors of the rainbow. He, too, waved to us, and we waved back.

I spied three small figures in the distance. As we approached, I recognized Miri, Klari, and Tamas. They were jumping up and down, waving their arms, yelling for us to stop the sleigh. I called to Papa, but he did not seem to hear me. Nor did Dezso. I leaned over Papa's shoulders and grabbed the reins out of his hands. I pulled on them hard, but the horses would not slow down.

Suddenly, somebody was shaking my arm. It was Mama. She was leaning over my bed. Her eyes were red.

"Wake up, lazy bones," she teased. "We still have time for a piano lesson before lunch."

Thursday, April 6, 1944

The next morning, I sat down at the piano to practice. The ordered notes soothed me. Later, I rewrote parts of my essay about Canada for Miss Szabo and copied it out in my best handwriting. By the afternoon, I was suffering from cabin fever. We were the only family with a phone, so I couldn't call Miri, but I knew she must be home because her mother wouldn't let her go to the shops. Like Mama, Mrs. Schwarz felt that it was too risky for a Jewish girl to leave the house on her own while bands of Arrow Cross men and German soldiers were patrolling the streets.

Despite Mama's cautions, I slipped out of the house while she and Grandmama were busy and ran across to Miri's. Nobody answered the doorbell. I banged on the door loudly. No answer. I tried again. When the door remained closed,

I headed back home. The window of Miri's bedroom faced the street. As I passed it, the corner of the lace curtain twitched, and for a moment I was staring into Miri's eyes. A hand appeared, and the curtain was lowered. I ran back to the door and rang the bell and knocked as loudly as I could, but nobody opened it.

When I got home, Mama was reading and Grandmama was unraveling an old sweater so she could reuse the yarn. I told them what had just happened.

Mama and Grandmama exchanged glances. Grandmama turned to me. "Have you thought that perhaps Miri and her mother have decided to –"

Mama interrupted her. "Grandmama!"

My head swiveled from one face to the other. "What?"

"Nothing," said Mama. "Absolutely nothing."

"I guess you're right." Grandmama stood up. "It's time to get supper started."

The minutes crawled by. I tried to read. I worked on the cross-stitch sampler for Papa's birthday, but I was so restless that I kept making mistakes and had to unpick my stitches over and over again until the cloth was grubby. At long last, the cuckoo in the grandfather clock called out four notes. I knew that Klari would be home from school, and there was still an hour left before curfew.

"I don't want you to go out," said Mama. "You might run into an Arrow Cross thug or one of the Germans and then who knows what would happen?"

"I've got to get out, Mama! I feel as if I'm in jail. Klari is just around the corner. I can't possibly get into trouble by going over to her place."

"I understand. You want to be with your friends." Mama faltered. "It's just that I couldn't bear it if anything happened to you." She paused. "All right. But promise me that you'll be careful and come right back."

"I promise," I said and left the room before she could change her mind.

The canary yellow star on my sweater made me feel as if the whole world were staring at me. I was careful not to look at any passersby and fixed my eyes on the ground.

I smelled a warm, spicy goulash as I knocked on Klari's front door. I hoped her mother would invite me to stay for an early supper. The door was opened a crack, and I saw Klari peering out at me with an expression I couldn't identify. She stepped outside and closed the door behind her.

"Let's stay here," she said. "My mother is cleaning and doesn't want us underfoot." I saw her glance at the star on my sweater and then quickly avert her gaze. She was chewing her lip, a sure sign that she was nervous.

"What's the matter with you?" I asked.

"I'm fine. I miss you and Miri."

"How was school?"

"The same. Dull without you. I hope you'll be back soon."

"Me too. It was so boring to be at home the whole day. Mama doesn't want me to go out." I handed her my essay. "I did Miss Szabo's assignment. Can you ask her to mark it?"

"Of course I will."

Tamas stepped outside. He was a Tamas I had never seen before, dressed in the green Arrow Cross uniform with its white armband with two arrows in the shape of a cross on it. I stared at this stranger, unable to speak. He stood there on the stoop, silent, staring back at me. Klari's nervous giggle broke the tension.

"Doesn't Tamas look stupid in his uniform?" she asked.

"Shut up, Klari!" He turned to me. "I'm sorry, Jutka," he said. "I had no choice. Father made me join the Arrow Cross."

"You did have a choice," said Klari. "You could have said no!"

"Father would have been furious. He believes the future of Hungary lies with the Arrow Cross. He says that all true patriots should join the party." He blushed a deep crimson. "Of course I don't agree with the party's policies about Jews, but we must take the good with the bad."

Before I could reply, Mrs. Kohegyi opened the door and looked out. She was a kind-faced woman, like a second mother to me.

"Jutka," she said, "I didn't know you were here! I am so sorry, but you've got to leave. Klari's father will be home any minute. He mustn't see you! Go away!"

Without another word, she pulled Tamas and Klari into the house and slammed the door in my face. I stood there for a moment, staring at the closed door. Then I ran home, crying the entire way.

Late that night, a loud noise from the street woke me. I looked out the window without turning on the light. A jeep was idling in front of Miri's house. Two men climbed out. Though the street was dark and the night sky was cloudy, I could tell they were wearing uniforms. One of them reached for the rifle slung over his shoulder and shot the lock off Miri's front door. The lights went on inside. I heard a loud crashing noise and saw Mrs. Schwarz's ornately carved settee sail through a window. It was followed by chairs and a small desk. After the men got back in the jeep, loaded with the Schwarzes' possessions, they drove off. The street became quiet again, as if only the dead lived there.

I ran to Mama's room and woke her. She sat up, rubbing her eyes.

"What's the matter?"

I told her what I had seen.

She listened to me, motionless, her hands clasped together so tightly that her knuckles turned white.

"Don't worry!" she finally said. "They'll be fine."

5

Monday, May 8, 1944

Mama came into the kitchen wearing her housecoat, her face wan and her hair hanging limply. Grandmama and I looked at her in alarm. Mama was always dressed, her hair carefully combed, before she appeared at the breakfast table.

"What's the matter, Kornelia? Are you sick?" asked Grandmama.

Mama forced a smile. "I'm fine, but I have a terrible headache." She poured herself a cup of coffee. "This should help."

"A migraine?"

Whenever Mama had one of her headaches, she felt so ill that she spent the entire day in a dark room with a wet compress over her eyes.

"My head aches terribly, but don't worry about it," she said. "I have to go to the store. We still have a coupon left, and Janos told me that he'll be getting a few kilos of cheese today. He said he'd try to put some of it aside for us, but there is only so much he can do with Kicsi looking over his shoulder. If I don't get there early, the cheese will be gone."

Mama had signed over the ownership of Papa's grocery store to his longtime clerk, Janos Nagy, after it became illegal for Jews to own a business. Janos tried to help us whenever he could. Ever since the Germans had occupied Hungary, we got fewer food ration coupons than Christians. And because of the curfew, by the time we got to the shops, the shelves were often bare. We depended on Janos's kindness for the bare necessities. But his helper, Istvan Kicsi, was a member of the Arrow Cross and spied on Janos. I knew he was waiting for the chance to denounce him.

"Kornelia, you cannot possibly go out," said Grandmama. "We'll manage without the cheese."

"We can't, Grandmama. Only three half-rotten potatoes are left in the pantry. I have to get us something to eat or we'll starve."

Grandmama said nothing. The grocery store was too far for her to walk.

"Grandmama is right. You're too sick to go out, Mama. I'll go to the store for you."

"Absolutely not, Jutka. It's not safe."

"I'll be careful. I promise. We have no choice. We need food, and you are in no shape to get it."

"The child is right. There is no other way," said Grandmama.

An hour later, I was on my way, a burlap shopping bag in my hand. I searched the streets for Arrow Cross or German soldiers. My luck held until I turned the corner to Papa's shop. A hooting crowd was clustered in front of the store. They were watching four Arrow Cross men beat up a man with a long beard. The garish yellow star on the poor wretch's jacket was visible even from a distance. I turned to go home, but a group of German soldiers was coming down the sidewalk, blocking my way. I lifted up the shopping bag and held it in front of my chest to hide the yellow star on my blouse and started back toward Papa's shop. When I got closer, I could hear the taunts of the Arrow Cross men as they kicked and punched their victim. The forlorn man raised his head. It was Rabbi Friedman.

I inched my way toward the open door of the shop, my bag still clutched to my chest. One of the Arrow Cross men grabbed Rabbi Friedman's long beard and yanked it with all his might. The rabbi fell to his knees. The Arrow Cross man looked up in triumph. It was Tamas. He saw me the instant I saw him. Our eyes locked. He opened his mouth and then closed it wordlessly. He looked away. I slipped into the grocery store.

Janos had been watching through the window. He pulled me behind the counter and pushed me down. Kicsi was in the crowd, but he hadn't seen me.

"Stay here! The bastards will soon be gone." Janos returned to his post by the window. I crouched on the wood floor, barely daring to breathe. Tamas's face, full of hate, swam in front of my eyes. I tried to think of something else. For an instant, I remembered how I used to play with my dolls in this exact spot when I was a little girl, while Papa waited on customers above my head. Then the image of Tamas was back again.

"They're finally leaving," Janos said, "and they're taking poor Rabbi Friedman with them. Come out from there, Jutka, before that lazy, good-for-nothing Kicsi remembers that he is supposed to be working here."

By the time Kicsi returned to the shop, I was standing in front of the counter, the block of cheese safely stowed in my bag.

"I am sorry, Jutka," said Janos loudly, making sure that Kicsi could hear him. "I sold all the cheese this morning."

"I couldn't come earlier because of the curfew."

Kicsi smirked.

"Not like the old times, is it?"

"Leave the girl alone!" said Janos. "You know as well as I do that her father was a good boss, always fair to us!"

Kicsi snorted and walked into the storeroom, slamming the door behind him. Janos pushed a loaf of bread into my hands.

"I'm sorry, but this is all I have left," he whispered.

"It's more than enough, Janos."

"What have you heard from Mr. Weltner and Dezso?" he asked.

"We're worried. They've stopped writing. Mama says they must be digging ditches in a place far from a post office, or perhaps they aren't allowed to write letters any longer."

Loud noises came from the storeroom. "You better go now, Jutka, before he comes back," said Janos. "Please give my regards to your mama and grandmama."

I ran all the way home. I was lucky. Nobody stopped me. Mama and Grandmama were standing by the window, waiting for me.

"Any problems?" asked Mama.

"Everything is fine. Janos sends his regards."

That evening, as we feasted on jacket potatoes with melted cheese and toasted rye bread, I remembered again the expression on Tamas's face.

6

Tuesday, May 9, 1944 —
Thursday, May 11, 1944

Posters appeared ordering Jews into a ghetto located between Bastya Street and Korwin Street. We had one week to find new lodgings there and to transport our belongings. Mama had friends who lived in the area, but none of them had room for us. They had relatives from other parts of the city moving in with them. We were desperate, until I thought of Agi Grazer.

"Her father is in the same forced labor regiment as Papa and Dezso. Perhaps Agi and her mother will have room for us?"

"My brilliant daughter!" Mama cried. "Let's go over to the Grazers' immediately and ask them."

Number 6 Petofi Street was a shabby house that would have fit into a corner of our large home.

"It's much smaller than I expected," Mama said.

"We have nowhere else to go."

"You're right." She sighed. "Ring the doorbell!"

Agi opened the door.

"Jutka! Mrs. Weltner! It's nice to see you. What are you doing here?" She ushered us into a tiny hall.

"We've come to see your mother," said Mama.

"She's in the parlor. Let me take you to her."

I could sense Agi's curiosity as she led us down the hall, past a modest kitchen. The door was open, and I saw two women cooking on an old-fashioned, wood-burning stove. The smell of sauerkraut made my nose twitch.

The parlor was a small room made even smaller by a large upright piano beside the window. Mrs. Grazer was ironing pillowcases on the dining-room table.

"Look who came to see us, Mother," said Agi. "Mrs. Weltner and Jutka want to speak to you."

"What can I do for you, Mrs. Weltner?" asked Mrs. Grazer in a reserved tone.

Mama explained that we needed a place to stay in the ghetto.

"I wish you would have come to me sooner," said Mrs. Grazer. "We have no room. My husband's cousins moved in with us yesterday. They're using Agi's bedroom and Agi's sharing my bed."

Mama's face fell. "You were our last hope, Mrs. Grazer. We have nowhere else to go." I could see that the words had not come easily.

"Mother, what about the parlor?" asked Agi. "If the police find out that we have an empty room, they'll force strangers on us."

Mrs. Grazer set the iron on its stand. "You're probably right, Agi." She turned to Mama. "If you think you can manage, Mrs. Weltner, you are welcome to stay in the parlor. You must bring your own beds with you. We don't have extras. And I must ask you to allow Agi to practice the piano."

Mama pumped Mrs. Grazer's hand enthusiastically. "Of course, Mrs. Grazer. At least she won't have to go far for her lessons."

The doorbell interrupted our dinner.

"Who could that be?" asked Mama. Her fingers tightened on her fork.

"It may be Klari," I offered. I hadn't seen Klari since her mother had slammed the door in my face. When Mama heard that Tamas had joined the Arrow Cross, she said it was too dangerous for me at their house. No matter how much I argued, she would not be dissuaded. I missed Klari terribly.

The doorbell rang again.

"It must be her!" I jumped up. "I'll get it!"

Mama put down her fork and knife. "I'll come with you."

"So will I," said Grandmama.

We crowded into the tiny foyer by the front door.

"We should open the door," said Mama, not moving.

I ran to the sitting room that faced the street and peeked through the curtains. Miss Szabo was on the front porch. She

43

was tapping her foot, her eyes restlessly searching the street.

I returned to the foyer and told Mama whom I had seen.

"What could she want?" Mama asked.

"Only one way to find out," said Grandmama.

"Open the door."

I lifted the latch.

"What a pleasant surprise," said Mama to Miss Szabo.

"May I come in?" Miss Szabo sounded frightened.

"Of course, of course," said Mama, pulling her into the hall and carefully latching the door behind her.

Miss Szabo followed us down the hall. She looked around the parlor.

"Can we be overheard, Mrs. Weltner?"

"There are only the three of us in the house," said Mama. "Please, sit down. Perhaps you'd like a cup of what passes for coffee nowadays?"

Miss Szabo shook her head.

Mama looked at her curiously. "It must be something important if you risked coming to see us."

"You're quite right. I want to discuss something with you, but first, I have to talk to Jutka."

She turned to me and began to speak. "Klari brought your assignment to me, Jutka, and I read it with great interest." She clasped my hands in hers. "You deserve to receive the certificate for the best story in the fifth form, but I can't give it to you. You also deserve to have your story displayed on the classroom wall for your friends to read, but I can't put it up." Her grip tightened until she was hurting my fingers.

"I am so sorry, my dear, but Principal Nemeth has forbidden me to give the prize to a Jewish student."

"It's not fair!" I broke away from her grasp.

Mama put her arm around me. It made me feel even worse.

"Of course it isn't fair, but it's very kind of Miss Szabo to let you know in person," she said.

"It breaks my heart not to be able to reward you. And I agree with the sentiments you expressed. I hope you will be able to rejoin us very soon." She dabbed her eyes with a handkerchief before taking my hand again. She was so distressed that I felt sorry for her. At the same time, my disappointment threatened to overwhelm me.

"I would appreciate it if you would not tell anyone about this conversation," Miss Szabo continued, "since it would cause problems for me if it became known that I visited you. I would certainly lose my job."

"I won't tell anybody."

She released my hands and turned to Mama.

"Mrs. Weltner," she said, "there is something I must speak to you about, but perhaps alone?"

"You can speak in front of Jutka," said Mama. "She has had to grow up over the last months, and I have no secrets from Grandmama."

"If you insist." Miss Szabo's voice dropped so low that we had to lean forward to hear her speak. "I am very sorry to hear that you and your family were ordered to move into the ghetto."

"So are we," said Mama. She exchanged puzzled looks with Grandmama.

Miss Szabo lowered her voice even more. "Mrs. Weltner, I believe that this order is the first of many more terrible ordinances to come. I have cousins in Germany, and I have heard some rumors. The Germans, with the help of the Arrow Cross, will deport you from Hungary."

"I was born in Hungary. So were my parents. I have my father's medal for bravery in the First World War. He fought on the side of the Germans."

"But, Mrs. Weltner –"

"We've heard the rumors too. We may be taken to a work camp. That's happened in Poland. If we have to go, we'll wait out the end of the war there. The war can't last forever."

Miss Szabo paced across the flowered carpet. "Work camp? You speak of work camps, Mrs. Weltner?" She stopped in front of Mama and leaned close. "Do you know what will happen to you? The Nazis will torture you, or worse!"

An expression of distrust flitted across Mama's face. She stood up. I could see by the flush in her cheeks how upset she was. "I expected more of you, Miss Szabo," she said evenly. "I would have thought that a woman of your intelligence would be the last person in the world to worry us with such nonsense!"

Miss Szabo caught hold of Mama's arm, but Mama shook off her hand and held the door open.

"It was kind of you to visit," she said. "Good-bye!"

"Fine, throw me out, but listen to me first," Miss Szabo pleaded. "Please, don't be offended by what I'm saying. My sources are trustworthy. I want to help you. My cousin owns the Petancy Water Works across the border in Austria. Two of his workers died recently in an accident. We'll put your photos into their workbooks. The Jews from that area have already been deported. If you go there, nobody will suspect you are Jewish."

"What about Grandmama?" I asked. "Can you get her papers too?"

"I am sorry, Madam," Miss Szabo said to my grandmother, "but nobody would believe that a person of your age works in a bottling factory."

"You are quite right, my dear," Grandmama said. "Kornelia, you must listen to Miss Szabo. This is an opportunity for both you and Jutka to get out."

"I refuse to listen to ridiculous, alarmist rumors," said Mama. "Nor would I dream of leaving you behind."

"What if the rumors are true?" Grandmama cried. "You must save yourself and Jutka!"

"Listen to Miss Szabo, Mama!" I said. "She must know what she is talking about . . . but we can't leave Grandmama."

Mama walked over to the window and stared outside for a long moment. Then she squared her shoulders and turned around, her expression set in stone.

"All of you are foolish," she said. "It's not possible for such horrible rumors to be true. I would never leave you behind, Grandmama, and Jutka, you are too young to go anywhere by yourself. What's more, how would Papa and Dezso find us when they return?"

We had no answers for her.

She turned to Miss Szabo. "Thank you for coming to see us. I know you mean well."

Miss Szabo looked defeated. "Is there anything I can say to change your mind?"

"Nothing," said Mama.

With a few words of farewell, she ushered Miss Szabo out of the house.

7

Tuesday, May 16, 1944 — Wednesday, May 17, 1944

Janos and his horse cart arrived in the tender spring dawn to transport our belongings to the ghetto. The parlor at Agi's house was so small that we could only bring along the absolute necessities. It had been difficult to decide what we couldn't bear to leave behind. Mama's old-fashioned, carved bed was so heavy that Janos couldn't carry it by himself. Mama and I grabbed one end while Janos hoisted the other. We pushed and shoved until we were finally able to get it into the buggy. As I leaned against the cart to catch my breath, I noticed Mr. Kristof watching us from his porch next door. I waved, but he turned on his heels and went inside without waving back.

"Forget him," Mama said. "People show their true colors in these terrible times. Let's get the rest of our things."

It didn't take long to fill the cart. In addition to Mama's bed, which she planned to share with Grandmama, we moved the mattress from my bed. We'd packed clothing, sheets, comforters, pillows, pots and pans, and the few supplies from our pantry.

"The cart is full," Janos said. "I'll make another trip."

"That's kind of you," Grandmama said, "but the parlor is so small that we don't have room for anything more."

"Is there something else you want to bring before I lock the door?" Mama asked me.

Before I could reply, I heard running footsteps. It was Klari. She bent over, panting, trying to catch her breath. "I didn't want you to go without wishing you good luck. I would have come sooner, but Father locks me in my room after school every day to stop me from coming to see you."

"How did you get out?"

She giggled. "The window."

"Your father will be furious."

"Never mind him. I have to show you something." She pulled a crumpled envelope out of her pocket and gave it to me. It was addressed to her, and the postmark was from Italy. "Read it," she said. "Father didn't give it to me when it arrived. I found it by chance on his desk when I was looking for something else."

I pulled the letter out of the envelope. It was a short note.

April 16, 1944
Somewhere in Yugoslavia

Dear Klari,

I wanted to let you know that we are safe. Papa won't allow me to tell you anything else.

Klari, it was safer to send this letter to you than to Jutka. Please let her read it. I miss both of you very much.

Love from your friend,
Miri

I felt as if a great weight had been lifted off my shoulders. "Thank God, Miri is all right!" I cried.

"I have to go home now before my father gets back," Klari said and hugged me again.

"Wait! Tell me who won the writing contest."

"It hasn't been announced yet. I really have to go." With a last embrace, she set off at full speed. "I'll come to see you!" she called over her shoulder.

"You're lucky to have such a loyal friend," said Mama.

"I know, Mama."

"Well, we should be going too." She took a key out of her pocket. "I'll lock up."

I helped Grandmama climb to the front seat of the buggy beside Janos. Mama and I set out on foot to Agi's. It was a beautiful day. The May sun was so warm that Mama kept wiping her forehead with her handkerchief. The street was eerily silent, curtains drawn. Nobody was outside calling for the children to come home. No one was sweeping the front steps. We were about to turn the corner when I grabbed Mama's arm.

"My Canada book! I forgot to bring my Canada book with me."

"Never mind! It'll be there when we go home."

"Please, Mama! Let me go back and get it. I don't want to leave it behind." Somehow it seemed important to have the book with me.

She sighed. "This is nonsense . . ."

"Please, Mama!"

She handed me the key to the house. "Don't be long! I'll wait for you here."

I ran back home. It was so quiet inside that I could actually hear my own ragged breathing. The Canada book was in its place on the top shelf of the bookcase above my desk. I tucked it under my arm and turned to leave. Before I closed the door, I looked back. I tried to memorize the way the sunbeams danced through the window, the color of the ink in the bottle on my desk, the brightness of the first cross-stitch sampler I ever made hanging above my bed. "Home Sweet Home," it read. It was the last thing I saw before I shut the door.

The parlor at Agi's house was even smaller than I remembered, but we knew we were lucky. We had somewhere to stay. Most of the floor space was taken up by Mama's bed. We had set it up under the window, next to the piano. My mattress was on the floor. There was no wardrobe, so we arranged our belongings in neat piles in a corner of the room. Mama placed photographs of Papa and Dezso on top of the piano. The room began to look like home.

The kitchen was down the hall. It was so tiny that there wasn't enough room in it for all of the cooks, so Mama, Grandmama, Mrs. Grazer, and the cousins drew up a cooking schedule.

By nightfall, we were exhausted. The mattress on the floor proved to be comfortable and I fell into a deep, dreamless sleep.

The next morning, Mama announced that she was going to give Agi and me a piano lesson. The little house was soon ringing with a four-handed Kodaly sonata. As we played, I thought about Castle Hill, sliding down the snow on a toboggan, with my arms tight around Tamas's body. The piece ended with a deep crescendo. Agi and I looked at each other without speaking. Joy flooded my heart, and I could see by Agi's expression that she felt the same way.

Mama walked over to the window and opened the curtains.

"It's a beautiful day," she exclaimed.

"I'll show you around the neighborhood, Jutka," Agi offered.

"I'd like to walk home to get more music books. It would be fun to practice different pieces together."

"That would be great," Agi said.

"I don't want you on the streets!" said Mama.

"We'll be fine, Mrs. Weltner. We'll be careful."

"All right, but don't be long."

Agi and I left before Mama could change her mind. We walked down Petofi Street, to Bastya Street, then over to Korona Street in the direction of my house. A tall wooden fence with barbed wire on top of it halted our progress.

"This wasn't here yesterday!" Agi cried. "They must have built it during the night."

Despite the soft May day, I shivered. "Let's try another way!" We went back to Bastya Street and walked to the very end. Again, we were stopped by a fence edged with barbed wire. Soon we were running up and down every crowded street in the ghetto. Each time we were stopped by a fence topped with barbed wire. Finally, in the middle of Kossuth Street, the very first street into the ghetto, we came upon a large gate guarded by armed policemen and several Arrow Cross men. One of them was Tamas. The Tamas I didn't know. The Tamas with the cold eyes.

I whispered, "Let's go back."

"Are you crazy? Tamas was in my class at school, and his sister is your friend. He'll let us out."

Before I could stop her, Agi walked up to him. I had no choice but to follow her.

"Hello, Tamas," she said cheerfully. "I haven't seen you for a long time. How are you doing?"

Tamas turned his head away and did not answer.

Agi plucked at his arm. "What's the matter with you?" she asked. "Jutka and I want to go to her house to fetch her piano music. We won't be long."

Tamas shook off her hand, walked over to one of his cronies, and whispered something in his ear. The policeman pulled his revolver from his holster and pointed it at Agi's head.

"Stop bothering us, Jewish bitches! Don't you understand that you can't leave the ghetto? Why do you think we put you here?" He waved his gun. "Now, get out of my sight while you still can!"

We ran as fast as we could. I thought that my heart would jump out of my chest. The laughter of the men at the gate echoed after us.

8

Tuesday, June 27, 1944 —
Wednesday, June 28, 1944

As the long warm days passed, Mama, Grandmama, and I clung to one another. Agi was not as fortunate. Her sweet and gentle mother was frail and had taken to her bed, not even bothering to eat. Agi had most of her meals with us. Her cousins kept to themselves in their room, and we only ran into them in the kitchen.

Mama taught Agi and me piano every morning. We took turns practicing. I spent the rest of the morning buried in my school books. I missed school, and especially Klari. Christians were not allowed into the ghetto without special visitors' passes.

The late June sun streaming into the room through the open windows and the chirping of the birds in the garden distracted me. I put away my school work and carried my

Canada book outside. I sat down on a wooden bench under a tall oak tree and leafed through the pictures of cowboys and Indian chiefs until I came upon the photographs of the busy modern streets full of people. I looked at the pictures carefully, studying each face and pretending I was among them. I was so absorbed that when Agi spoke to me I jumped.

"What are you reading?" she asked.

I held out the book to her. She sat down beside me.

"*Canada*," she said, reading the title.

"My papa's cousin lives in Canada. She sent us this book."

She began turning the pages, exclaiming over the photographs. "Look at all that space!"

"Turn to the last few pages."

She gazed at the wide streets lined with tall buildings. "The people in the pictures look so happy," she said. "Nobody is wearing a star."

"When the war is over, I'm going to Canada."

She grinned at me. "I'll come with you."

"Promise?"

"Promise."

The back door opened, and Mama came into the garden. Grandmama was right behind her, her arm through Mrs. Grazer's arm. Mama was carrying Grandmama's wooden stool.

"It's such a lovely day," Mama said, "much too nice to stay indoors. We convinced Kati to come outside with us."

57

"I didn't want to disappoint you, my dear," said Mrs. Grazer, "although I don't feel up to it."

"You are reading your Canada book again," said Mama. "Aren't you getting bored with it?"

Before I could reply, Mrs. Grazer reached for the book. "Let me see it." She turned the pages slowly. "How I wish that we lived there! I've heard that nobody ever goes hungry in Canada."

"Jutka and I are going to visit Canada after the war," Agi said. "Will you come with us, Mother? And Father too?"

"I promised Jutka that her papa and I will go with her," said Mama. "Dezso will want to come along too. Canada is such a beautiful country. It'll be nice to see Armin's cousin."

"I'm too old," said Grandmama. "I'll have to hear about Canada secondhand."

"I'm not well enough to travel," said Mrs. Grazer. "As for your father, Agi . . . he'd never leave me."

Agi's face fell.

"I am still going to go, Mother." Agi was determined.

"You might change your mind, Kati," said Mama.

Mrs. Grazer shook her head. She broke a leafy branch off a bush and fanned herself.

"Let's talk about this another time," said Mama. She looked around the sun-dappled garden. "What a lovely day!" she repeated. "If only Armin and Dezso were with us!"

"And my Fritzi too," added Mrs. Grazer. "It worries me that we haven't heard from them for so long."

"And Jonah," Agi added. She jumped up. "I'll get my camera and take our picture. We can send our photographs to our fathers. Just because they haven't been able to write to us doesn't mean they won't receive our photos!"

"Have you lost your mind, my daughter?" said Mrs. Grazer. "If the authorities discover that you didn't hand in your camera when you were supposed to, you'll be deported!"

"How would they ever find out, Mother?" Agi asked. "Nobody can see over the fence, and I'll develop the photographs myself. Father's darkroom is still set up in the cellar."

I could tell that Mrs. Grazer was frightened, but she said, "I guess it should be all right, but I don't want my picture taken." She patted the back of her head. "My hair isn't tidy."

Agi ignored her. I took my Canada book out of Mrs. Grazer's hand and gave it to Agi, who went back into the house.

I moved over on the bench to make room for the others and helped Grandmama put her feet on top of the wooden stool.

"Much better," she said.

Agi came outside, carrying a large old-fashioned camera and a tripod. "I only have enough film for two pictures, and the film is very old. The photos might not even turn out."

"Let's see what happens," I said. "I'll take a picture of you, Agi, and you can send it to Jonah."

Agi blushed fiery red as she stood in front of the wrought-iron gate. She looked pretty in her short-sleeved print dress. She had copied the hairstyle of the American movie star

Judy Garland, with her long hair flowing over her shoulders and a large sausage curl at her forehead.

"Take my picture here, with the fence and the house in the background," she said.

I snapped her photo.

"Thank you, Jutka," she said. "Now perhaps Jonah won't forget me. It's your turn next. Stand behind my mother and I'll take your picture."

"Absolutely not!" cried Mrs. Grazer. "I'll be the photographer. I can't possibly have my photo taken today without any lipstick or powder and my hair like a rat's nest. I don't want Fritzi to see me like this."

"You're being silly, Kati," said Mama. "As long as Fritzi can see your picture, he won't care about your hairstyle."

When we saw that there was no convincing Agi's mother, Agi handed her the camera and took her spot on the bench. I stood behind them, my hands resting on Grandmama's shoulders, grinning from ear to ear.

"Well, that's the end of the film," said Agi after her mother took the picture. "I'll develop the photos tonight."

The next morning, Agi showed me the photographs.

"They're blurry," I said.

"I told you they might not turn out. The film is old, but there is no way of getting new film these days."

"Let me see." Grandmama held the photographs carefully. "Your papas and Dezso and Jonah won't care how clear the pictures are as long as they can see you." She shook her head. "Agi, I do wish that your mother would have allowed herself to be photographed."

"So do I," Agi said, "but once Mother makes up her mind about something there is no changing it." She gave a small, rueful laugh. "I showed her the pictures this morning. She is still in bed." She turned to me. "Where is your mother? I'd like to show her the photos."

"She went for a walk. She should be back soon."

As if on cue, the door burst open. Mama, her face pale, clutched a sheet of paper in her hand.

"What's the matter? What's wrong?" Agi asked.

Mama sank down on a chair, gasping. "This announcement is all over the walls of the ghetto." She handed the paper to Grandmama. Grandmama read it and passed it to me:

THE ENTIRE JEWISH POPULATION
OF PÁPA IS ORDERED TO
REPORT TO THE MAIN GATE OF
THE JEWISH GHETTO
TOMORROW, JUNE 29, 1944, AT 8 A.M.
EACH PERSON IS ALLOWED ONE PIECE
OF LUGGAGE, MAXIMUM WEIGHT 15 KG.
ANYONE DISOBEYING THIS ORDER
WILL BE SHOT!

The order was signed by the police chief, Principal Nemeth's cousin.

"Well, it was to be expected," said Grandmama tartly. "We knew that it would happen sooner or later. We are better off somewhere else than in this filthy, overcrowded ghetto. But it'll be difficult to leave the last of our things behind."

"How will Papa find us when he comes back?" Mama fretted.

"How will Jonah find me?" Agi cried. "He'll forget me! I won't be able to send him my photo!"

"He won't forget you! He'll remember you, just as you remember him." I knew my words were useless.

Grandmama put her arm around Mama's shoulders. "Don't worry, Kornelia! The authorities will know where we've been moved. I know my son. He'll find us somehow."

"Papa will have no trouble finding us!" I sounded childish, even to my own ears. "We don't have much time to get ready. We better plan what to take with us."

9

Thursday, June 29, 1944 — Friday, June 30, 1944

That evening, we stowed most of our money and jewelry into a flat metal box that we buried in the cellar, except for the thick gold bracelet Papa had given Mama as a wedding gift. She never took it off. Agi and her mother buried their valuables beside ours. They stashed Mrs. Grazer's Persian lamb coat and their silver candlesticks into a suitcase and left it behind the coal bin.

We climbed upstairs, too sad to speak. Agi and her mother went to their room. Mama locked the door of the parlor.

"There is something else I have to do," said Mama. She lifted up a corner of the mattress and pulled out a small cardboard cigar box that held a dozen gold coins. "Papa gave me this money before he left. He told me I should always keep the coins with me. I'm going to hide them in the lining of my winter jacket."

Grandmama helped her unpick the lining around the collar of the camel-hair coat. Then Mama stitched the coins to the material. Each one was held in place by a large cross-stitch. Then she sewed the lining back in place. The fur collar covered the bulge.

We spent hours deciding what else to pack. It was midnight by the time we went to bed. I was so exhausted that I fell asleep immediately. At dawn, the doorbell woke me. Mama and Grandmama sat bolt upright in their bed. Agi and her mother appeared in the doorway.

"What now? Who could it be?" Mama clutched Grandmama's arm. "Don't open the door. Maybe they'll go away."

"It must be important or they wouldn't wake us up at such an hour!" Mrs. Grazer said.

We went to the front hall, past the cousins' closed bedroom door.

"A cannon wouldn't wake those two," said Agi. The doorbell rang again.

I opened the door a crack. Standing on the stoop, wrapped in an enormous black scarf, was Julia, Mrs. Grazer's housekeeper. Julia had been with Agi's family forever, until the government had made it illegal for Christians to work in Jewish homes. Julia's wide face shone pale in the early morning light and she looked around nervously. Agi pulled her into the house and kissed her cheek.

"Julia, it's so good to see you! What are you doing here? How did you get into the ghetto?"

"I bribed the guards." Julia smiled and took Mrs. Grazer's arm. "Oh, Madam, I had to come and see you when I heard they were taking you away! I wanted to say good-bye."

She shrugged the scarf off her shoulders and revealed a wicker basket. She unpacked three long sticks of salami, two loaves of bread, and six red apples. "You'll need to eat something. I wish I could have brought you more, but this was all I could spare."

"Julia, my dear, please don't apologize," Mrs. Grazer said. "This is a feast these days. Thank you so much for your kindness."

"Can I eat one of the apples, Mother?" asked Agi. "I'm starving."

"Absolutely not! We must save them for our journey. But, first, let me give Jutka and her family their share. I'll give your father's cousins their portion tomorrow." She laughed. "They'll sleep through anything!" She began to divide the rations in three.

"Kati, this food is for you and Agi," said Mama. "We wouldn't dream of taking it away from you."

"We want to share it with you," insisted Mrs. Grazer. "I know that Agi has been having many of her meals with you. I am glad to have the opportunity to repay you."

"Well, if you put it like that, Kati, we'll be very happy to accept your generosity."

Julia wiped her eyes. "Oh, Madam, it's just like you to be so kind. I will never forget how good you were to me. I wish I could do more for you!"

"There *is* something else you could do for us, Julia," said Agi. "Could you keep Mama's coat until we come home? And our candlesticks?"

Agi fetched the suitcase from the cellar, and Julia wrapped the candlesticks in the fur coat. She stroked the soft fur with her calloused fingers.

"I'll take good care of it, Madam," she promised, "and the candlesticks too. I know how much they mean to you." She turned to Mama. "Do you want to give me something for safekeeping, Mrs. Weltner? Grandmama?"

"Give your bracelet to Julia, Mama."

Mama's hand reached to undo the clasp, but then she hesitated. "I can't bear to give it up. When I look at it, I always think of your papa."

"They'll just take it away from you, Mama!"

"I'll wear a dress with long sleeves. Nobody will see it."

"Are you sure that you don't want me to hide it for you, Mrs. Weltner?" asked Julia. "I promise to keep it safe."

"Thank you, my dear, but I don't want to part with it."

There was no changing Mama's mind. But I gave Julia my Canada book. Agi slipped the two photographs she had taken yesterday between the pages.

Mrs. Grazer turned to Julia. "We appreciate your kindness, my dear, but you must leave before the guards at the gates are changed."

We helped Julia wrap herself in her scarf and bade her good-bye with many tears.

"We'll see you soon," said Mrs. Grazer.

"The war will be over before long," added Grandmama.

"From your mouths to God's ears." The door quietly clicked closed behind Julia.

Even though it was early in the morning, the summer sun was relentless in the cloudless sky. Sweat trickled down my back, and the hair at the nape of my neck was damp. My heart pounded an erratic tippety-tap, tippety-tap at the sight of dozens of policemen with drawn rifles who quickly surrounded the subdued crowd of five thousand Jewish women, children, and a few old men. For the first time, I was glad that Papa and Dezso were with their forced labor regiment. Frail grandmothers were perched on stacks of luggage piled high on the dusty ground while terrified young mothers rocked their babes. Children ran back and forth. Many of the women were wearing their prettiest dresses and high heels, as if they were going to a tea party. However, we'd decided to put on our most comfortable clothes and sturdy shoes. I had a big suitcase, so heavy that I had to drag it along the ground. It was filled with our best clothing and Mama's jacket with the coins sewn into the lining.

Mama was bent low under the weight of the large knapsack we had fashioned out of a bedsheet. It contained our blankets and the food Mrs. Grazer had given us. The gold bracelet on her wrist was hidden by the long sleeve of her thin dress.

"It's more important to take food than extra clothing," said Mama. "You never know when they'll feed us next."

"Or what they'll feed us," added Grandmama darkly.

Because of her heart condition, doctors had forbidden my grandmother to lift anything. Last night, a terrible argument had ensued between my mother and grandmother, for Grandmama had insisted that she wanted "to do her share." After much begging and crying, Mama had prevailed, and Grandmama was carrying only a bulky burlap shopping bag that held her wooden stool.

We waited, numb, by the barbed-wire fence that enclosed the ghetto. A gang of raucous Arrow Cross men saw us and laughed at our distress. I spotted Tamas. As soon as he saw me looking at him, he turned away and did not glance at us again.

Agi and her mother appeared in the crowd. Mrs. Grazer was distraught. Her coiffed hair had escaped the confines of its bun, and her blue frock was badly rumpled.

"What will become of us? What will become of us?"

"Please, Mother, please! Calm down. Get hold of yourself," begged Agi.

Mama patted Mrs. Grazer's arm. "Kati, my dear, everything will be fine, just fine. You'll see," she soothed, speaking slowly as though to a child. She sounded as if she were trying to convince both Mrs. Grazer and herself.

"Where are your cousins?" I asked Agi.

She shook her head and pointed to the throng around us. "We were separated from them."

One of the policemen rattled the barbed-wire fence with the barrel of his rifle. We fell silent.

"It's Lajos Magyar, the chief of police," said Mama. "He used to be one of our customers. He is a fool, just like his cousin," and she pointed to Principal Nemeth glowering behind him.

"Dangerous fools," said Grandmama.

"Attention!" The chief puffed out his chest like a threatening ape.

"Where are you taking us?" called out a young woman, her head covered by a babushka.

"What will happen to us? What will happen to us?" moaned Mrs. Grazer. Agi hushed her.

"Silence!" cried the police chief. "Anybody interrupting me will regret it. You will be informed of your final destination in due course. There is no need for panic. There is no need for hysteria. You will be taken to a place where you will have to work hard for the first time in your miserable lives. You will be well treated, have plenty to eat, and you will be reunited with your husbands, fathers, and sons shortly after your arrival."

The crowd of desperate women gave a collective sigh of relief. I felt joy flooding my heart. To see Papa and Dezso again!

"Jonah might be there too," said Agi.

"They must be taking us to a work camp in Austria," guessed Mama. "They must have moved your papa and Dezso there before us." She squeezed my hand.

The chief banged the barrel of his rifle against the fence once again. "We will escort you to the old fertilizer factory just outside of town. You will leave from there."

"But, Chief Magyar, the fertilizer factory is at least an hour's walk from here. How do you expect us to go so far in this heat, laden down with our luggage?" cried the woman wearing the babushka.

Chief Magyar pointed his finger at Principal Nemeth, then nodded his head in the woman's direction. Nemeth walked up to the woman, and without even giving her a chance to shield her face with her hands, he hit her in the mouth with the butt of his gun. The woman made a gurgling sound and crumpled to the ground like a torn paper doll. An old woman next to her began keening like a wounded animal.

The hopeful mood of the crowd dissipated like a puff of smoke. In silence, we picked up our bundles and followed the police chief out of the ghetto. When I looked back, the yard was empty except for the body of the young woman with her suitcase standing lonely guard beside her.

We were thirsty and exhausted as we trudged along the deserted, dusty road in the overwhelming heat. Some of the women found their luggage so heavy that they left it by the wayside. Anybody who lagged behind earned a vicious kick from a policeman's boot. Mama and I linked arms with Grandmama and dragged her along with us, each of us carrying a bag with our free hand. Mrs. Grazer's arm was linked with Agi's.

A platoon of gendarmes in green uniforms with plumed hats and drawn rifles was waiting for us at the derelict fertilizer factory. Chief Magyar handed us over to Chief Gendarme Szucs, known far and wide for his cruelty. As Szucs and his minions herded us into the ruined building, I saw Tamas again. His expression was blank.

The fertilizer factory had been empty for years. Most of the roof had rotted away and dirty straw lined the mud floor. The walls of the cavernous interior room were filthy. There were no toilets, just reeking outhouses. Double railway tracks ran right through the center of the gigantic hall.

More gendarmes were waiting for us inside. No matter where we turned, a gun was pointed at our heads. Hungary was at war, but the guns were in the hands of our fellow Hungarians. We were lined up and ordered to hand over all of our valuables. There was no use resisting. When it was our turn, it was our misfortune to have Gendarme Szucs interrogating us. He pulled the clothing out of my suitcase.

"You can keep this!" he barked as he kicked the case back to me. Quickly, I stuffed everything in. "Have you any valuables? You better give them to me or you'll be sorry!"

Mama looked down at her wrist. I put my arm around her waist and my head on her shoulder. I whispered, "Give him the bracelet."

Mama gently pushed me away and faced Szucs. "I have a bracelet, sir," she said, slowly rolling up the sleeve of her dress. The bracelet shone bright on her wrist.

"Take it off!"

I was proud that Mama did not beg him to be allowed to keep it. She fumbled with the lock. I had to help her loosen it. The bracelet fell with a loud thunk on the table in front of Szucs. When he snatched it up, I noticed that his fingernails were caked with dirt. He looked around the room furtively and stuffed it into his pocket.

"The old bitch is next!" he yelled. "What are you carrying in your bag, old woman?"

Without a word, Grandmama emptied the contents of her sack. The wooden stool clattered onto the table.

"This will come in handy as firewood," said Szucs.

He was about to throw it into a large box on the floor by his feet when desperation overcame my fears. "Please, sir," I said as humbly as I could, "let us keep my grandmother's stool. She has a heart condition. She needs to elevate her feet or they swell up."

Szucs's face grew crimson and the veins in his forehead bulged alarmingly. "Keep your mouth shut!"

"Please, sir, what's a favor among friends?" Deliberately, I looked directly at the pocket of his pants into which Mama's bracelet had disappeared. I patted my own pocket. He turned even redder. For a moment I feared that he would grab me by the throat, but he leaned back in his chair.

"Get out of my sight!" he spat. I took the stool. He waved us away without checking Mama's knapsack.

"You're a brave girl," said Grandmama.

"At least we won't starve – for now," said Mama. Her eyes were bright with tears. "What will Papa say when he finds out that my bracelet is gone?"

"He'll buy you another one when the war is over," said Grandmama.

Next, we were lined up for a humiliating body search.

That night, our reserve of dry salami and bread long gone, we tossed and turned as we tried to sleep on the prickly hay. We were jarred awake by the screams of women, children, and old men who were being beaten most cruelly for withholding prized possessions. Early the next morning, the chug-chug of a steam engine pulling a long line of cattle cars woke me from a fitful sleep. The train came through the gates right into the fertilizer factory.

II

Hell

IO

Friday, June 30, 1944 —
Monday, July 3, 1944

I could sense the fear that ran through the crowd of terrified women and bewildered children as they caught sight of the train. The gendarmes yelled at us to line up in rows of five, and then they prodded, kicked, and shoved us into the cattle cars. Seventy or eighty people were herded into each cattle car that would have comfortably held thirty. Mama and I sat on the floor, leaning against her suitcase. Grandmama was leaning awkwardly against her wooden stool. She was the one suffering the most, but she did not utter a word of complaint. Only the pallor of her lips bore testament to her pain.

I felt faint from the press of sticky bodies against my skin, the stench of human flesh, and the staleness of the air in the overcrowded box. The summer sun cutting through the barred window high up on the wall of the car was so intense that I felt my bones would melt.

Before long, my muscles were screaming for relief. Every inch of the floor was taken up by human bodies except for a circle around two pails at opposite ends of the car. One pail was empty. The tepid drinking water that had filled it was long gone. The other pail was the toilet.

"I'd die before I'd use that bucket with all these people looking on," I said to Agi.

"We might not have a choice," she answered.

She was right. Some of the younger women piled their luggage around the pail to create an illusion of privacy and dignity for the poor wretches who had to use the bucket.

At first, people chatted to help pass the time. Young mothers comforted their crying children and soothed their restless babies. Agi had a wonderful singing voice. She stood on top of her suitcase and began to sing a song we'd learned at school. The wagon resonated with sweet voices as women and children joined in:

> Far, far away is my homeland,
> How I wish to see it once again.
> Windows with geraniums,
> How I wish that I was at home again.

Agi's pure notes broke at the end of the song. In the silence of the next moment, we remembered what we had lost, until Mrs. Grazer's lament brought us back to reality.

"What will happen to us? What will happen to us?"

As time crawled by, no one had the strength to talk. I sat scrunched up or lay crookedly in the gloom hour after monotonous hour. My mind began to play tricks on me. I began to imagine the wooden sides of the cattle car and its ceiling moving in closer and closer, pressing my body tighter and tighter against the other bodies, until all our flesh was melded into one flesh, and the cattle car became a traveling communal coffin.

The train slowly rolled through the countryside, stopping randomly in the middle of the fertile wheat fields. Whenever this happened, the people closest to the doors beat on them with all of their might but to no avail. The doors stayed closed, and one of the buckets remained empty while the other filled to overflowing with its foul contents.

I felt a raging thirst. My whole being was concentrated on the desire for a drink. I would have given anything, done anything, just to feel for an instant the cool, refreshing slipperiness of water on my tongue.

It was growing dark outside. We could only see patches of dusky sky through the barred window. The train suddenly stopped and the doors were flung open. Three Germans in black SS uniforms appeared in the open doorway, their rifles aimed at us. A few paces behind them stood a Hungarian peasant with a handlebar mustache. He was dressed in traditional wide pantaloons.

"Oh my God . . . Germans!" whispered Mama. "They must be handing us over to the Germans."

"We're in Kassa!" said Grandmama, pointing to a large sign hanging on the station wall. Kassa was on the Slovakian border.

"Where could they be taking us?" I asked my mother. "Didn't Chief Magyar say we were going to a work camp?"

Mama shook her head helplessly. "They're all liars."

A blond ss soldier, with the face of a bulldog, stepped forward. "Buckets! Give buckets!" he snarled in broken Hungarian.

We passed the two buckets to him, and he handed them to the peasant, who took them away. Then the three ss men stepped back, their rifles still pointed at us, and the doors of the cattle car clanged shut.

"They must be getting water for us. That's why they wanted the buckets," somebody said.

We waited and waited, but the Germans did not return. Finally, the door of the car was partially opened, and the ss man with the bulldog face reappeared just long enough to throw in an empty pail, narrowly missing a woman. The wagon doors banged shut again.

"Water! Water! Please! Give us water! Open the door! We need water!"

We pounded on the doors, but no one came. Mama and Grandmama were slumped over our luggage, eyes closed. I was desperate to look outside to see what was happening.

The wagon was so crowded that it was impossible to walk, so I crawled over prone, complaining bodies. A mound of luggage was piled up below the window. Someone gave me a boost so I could see the entire station. The normalcy of the scene stunned me. Nearby, two peasants were sitting on a wooden bench in front of the station house. One was munching on dark bread. He took a knife out of his pocket and cut off a slice. My mouth watered as I watched him offer it to his companion. A well-dressed couple with their little son stood on the platform waiting for a train. The young husband was leaning toward his wife, and her head was thrown back in laughter. The boy was hanging on to his mother's skirt as if his life depended on it. There were Hungarian soldiers, gendarmes, and ss men everywhere, chatting and laughing, as if they belonged to a different species than the cruel trio that had just left us.

The swishing sound of steam being released made me look down the tracks. Separated from our train by half-a-dozen railway tracks was a locomotive being filled with water. Long hoses attached to taps on the side of the station house were pouring water into an open valve on the top of the engine, making it come to life with hissing and rattling noises. I couldn't take my eyes off the throbbing engine slaking its thirst. I licked my parched lips. At first, I was filled with envy of the drinking monster, and then I was consumed by a greater grief than I have ever felt as I realized to what depths I had been reduced.

Two men in overalls and peaked caps were talking next to the locomotive. I forced my arms through the bars on the window and waved at them.

"Water! Please, please, give me some water!" I called.

One of the men looked in my direction. He stooped down and picked something up from the ground. I couldn't see what it was because the thick hoses obscured my line of vision. I felt faint with relief. He must have been picking up a container to fill it up with water for me. Suddenly, he pitched the object my way. A searing pain tore through my arm, and I fell backward onto the human carpet below me. It must have been a stone. My arm ballooned up and turned purple later on.

As we traveled through the dark countryside, only an occasional moan or cry interrupted the stillness. The blackness of the night outside mirrored our deepening desperation. When dawn finally stole into the wagon, it cast bars of shadow onto our faces.

"How long can this go on?" asked Grandmama softly. She hadn't spoken since we left Kassa.

"Not long, I hope," replied Mama. "We can't last much longer like this."

Agi nodded. Her mother was silent, her eyes blank.

The train rolled on and on through the wheat fields under a scorching, merciless sun. Day turned into night and night into day again before we arrived at another railway station. A sign in black letters read, AUSCHWITZ. We remained in the cattle car without moving for a full day. We waited and waited, but the doors of the wagon did not open. We were silent, too weak to protest. At noon the next day, the locomotive came to life again. A half-hour later, the train stopped, and the doors of the cattle car clanged open. The sudden brightness blinded me. I shook my head and rubbed my eyes. Several figures dressed in striped pajamas with matching caps appeared in the doorway. They were followed by a dozen German soldiers in the SS uniform. Their rifles were pointed at us.

"Los! Los! Out! Out!" they yelled.

Monday, July 3, 1944

Petrified. Turned to stone. Everything happened so fast that I had no time to think. I understood nothing. Who were the men in the striped pajamas? What did the Germans want from us? They were armed, so there was no choice but to obey their shouted orders: "Los! Los! Raus! Raus!"

An officer stepped forward. "Do not panic! You're in a good place." He sounded friendly, and he spoke perfect Hungarian. "You will be given food, water, and a comfortable bed to sleep in. You will be reunited with members of your families who were transported before you." A happy murmur broke through the crowd. Suddenly, without warning, the man screamed, "Los! Los! Get out of here!"

We linked arms with Grandmama and helped her climb down. I was holding her stool in my free hand. The men in the striped pajamas tossed our suitcases out of the train.

"My coat!" cried Mama. "I must get my coat back!"

"Forget it, Mama! Don't call attention to yourself. It's gone."

One of the men in stripes tried to take Grandmama's stool away from me.

"Please, sir! Let me keep it!" I pleaded. "My grandmother has a heart condition. She has to put her feet up so they don't swell. She might need her stool."

"She won't need it where she is going," he muttered in Hungarian, but he let go of it. Sweat ran down my face and trickled down my back. The cruel brightness of the sun highlighted Grandmama's pinched expression and the whiteness of her lips. It etched every line in Mama's tired face, making her look much older than her forty years. I was so exhausted and weak that I had to lean against the train.

"Hold on, Jutka," said Mama. "We'll soon get something to eat and a comfortable bed. And we'll see Papa and Dezso!"

Grandmama wasn't listening. She was looking around. "We must be in hell!" she said.

There was barbed wire everywhere. Men in ss uniforms and high shiny boots held the leashes of snarling dogs. Two watchtowers loomed behind us. Brick huts stood to our left and rows of wooden stables to our right. Ahead, several tall chimneys were belching black smoke into the air. An acrid, burning smell filled our lungs, making it difficult to breathe. Agi and I covered our noses with our hands.

"Men and women separate! The women's group goes first, with the men following them, five prisoners in each row!"

The guns pointed at us were incentive enough for us to move through the steps of this strange dance quickly and quietly. The eerie silence on the platform was only interrupted by the wails of young children in their mothers' arms and the barking of the dogs. I walked beside Grandmama, her stool still clutched in my hand. Mama was next to Agi and her mother.

A few minutes later the same officer yelled, "Form a single line!"

Mama went first. Behind her was Grandmama, then Mrs. Grazer, me, and Agi. We passed in front of an ss officer standing on a slightly elevated podium. He was a youngish man, tall and handsome. He held a short rubber stick. As the people passed him, he pointed his baton in the direction each person was supposed to go. Mama tried to tell him that the five of us were together. He did not answer her but pointed to the left. Mama obeyed his order. As Grandmama went by him, he pointed in the same direction. Mama slowed her steps to allow Grandmama to catch up to her. They joined the large group heading toward the belching chimneys. They looked back, trying to see where the rest of us were being sent. Mrs. Grazer was ordered left and followed them. Then it was my turn. *Please, God, please, God, let me go with Mama and Grandmama!* The ss officer's eyes raked over me, head to toe.

"Please, sir! Please, sir! Let me go with my mother and grandmother," I begged.

"How old are you, girl?" he asked. A man in stripes, standing behind him, translated.

I opened my mouth to tell him I was fourteen years old.

"Tell him that you are sixteen," the translator said to me in Hungarian before I could speak.

I did as he said. I held up all ten of my fingers, then six more.

The baton pointed to the right.

I obeyed. There was nothing else I could do. I saw that Mrs. Grazer had caught up with Mama and Grandmama just as Agi was sent to my group. I suddenly realized that I was still holding on to Grandmama's wooden stool. I could see the three women in the distance, near the back of the crowd.

"I'll be right back," I told Agi. "I have to give the stool to Grandmama!"

Without thinking, I ran after them. The ss guards did not stop me. The three women were walking slowly, with arms linked.

"You forgot the stool!" I gave it to Mama to carry.

"Be careful!" Grandmama said.

I turned around and ran back to my group. It didn't occur to me to kiss them good-bye or to stay with them. Mama's quiet "I love you!" followed after me floating in the foul air.

I2

Monday, July 3, 1944 – Tuesday, July 4, 1944

The SS herded us to the right, toward a building about a hundred meters away. We passed an inmate pushing a cart piled high with dead bodies. Bile rose in my throat.

"What *is* going on here? Grandmama was right. We *are* in hell!"

Agi did not reply, but the man with the cart must have heard me. He stopped and turned to us, his feverish eyes boring into my face. "See there?" he cackled in Hungarian, pointing to the chimneys in the distance. "Your families are going up in smoke! There goes your mama and your papa! Be careful or they'll get you too!"

We stared after him as he was swallowed by the crowd.

"He must be crazy!" Agi said. "What *is* he talking about?"

I had no answers.

We continued on for another fifty meters before stopping in front of the building where some men and women in striped clothing waited with large shears in their hands. The SS ordered us to undress, put our shoes at the side of the building, and add our clothes to a small mountain of garments piled next to the shoes. A few girls began to weep and tried to cover their nakedness with their hands. I felt nothing. It was as if everything was happening to somebody else, not to me. I just stood there, as if I were watching the plot of a bizarre movie unfolding before my eyes. I looked on calmly as the dark hair of a girl in the film dropped to the ground. The wailing of the women around me was muted in my ears, as if the sound were coming through a long tunnel. I didn't recognize the weeping stranger with a shorn blond head clinging to my arm.

"Oh, Jutka, what is happening to us?" she cried. It was Agi.

Then we were led into the bathhouse. The ceiling of the large hall was dotted with shower heads. Icy water began pouring out of them, but I barely felt the stinging cold beating down on me.

We left the shower room, naked, our bodies still dripping with water. The SS ordered us to run past a pile of dirty, ragged striped uniforms. A prisoner standing beside the pile threw a striped skirt, a tattered shirt, and a pair of men's shoes at me. I was lucky. The clothing fit, and the shoes were only slightly large. Agi's uniform was several sizes too small for her, and her shoes were wooden. She was able to trade her uniform for a larger one, but nobody would exchange her clogs for shoes.

Night was falling by the time we were marched at gun-point to the wooden barracks behind the barbed-wire fence. Agi and I clung to each other, determined to stay together. The long line of exhausted women was eerily quiet, until a whisper traveled through the crowd like wildfire through dry prairie grass. "Don't touch the fence! It's electrified!" Only then did I notice the white posters of skulls hanging on the fence.

The guards used their truncheons and whips to push and shove groups of women inside each building. Finally, it was our turn.

"They must think that we're animals! This is no better than a stable!" she said.

The cavernous room was dimly lit by skylights. Once my eyes adjusted to the darkness, I saw wooden rafters and an earth floor. On either side of the room were long lines of three-tiered bunk beds made of rough wood. Each bed frame was covered by a piece of plywood on which rested a filthy straw-filled burlap bag.

A young blond woman with the face of an angel ordered us to choose beds. She was wearing a striped uniform with a green triangle on her shirt. "Los! Los!" she cried harshly, waving her rubber stick. Within minutes, a thousand women were packed into the bunks. There were eight prisoners per bed, which was only meant for two. Elbows jabbed elbows, knees knocked knees, eliciting angry protests at the forced intimacy.

Agi and I held on to each other silently. There was nothing to say. We could hear the buzz of soft voices as the women tried to make themselves comfortable.

"Haltet die Klappe! Shut up!" cried the blond woman with the green triangle. She spoke in Hungarian. "I am your Kapo. Listen to me carefully. You're in Auschwitz-Birkenau. This is not a sanatorium! You are in a Vernichtungslager! You are Häftlings, prisoners. You will do exactly as you are told or you'll pay the consequences for your actions! Anybody who disobeys will go straight to the ovens! Understood?" Silence. "Now, all of you – outside! Line up in rows of five!"

I did not think. I did not question. Neither did Agi or any of the others. We scrambled back down. Each of us was given a rusty metal bowl and a spoon. Another line-up followed the first. A prisoner standing by a black metal cauldron dished thin soup into my bowl. A piece of turnip, the type farmers used to feed their cattle, floated on top of the murky liquid. The brew gave off a putrid odor that turned my stomach.

"I can't drink this slop! It'll make me vomit. I'm going to dump it."

"Don't you dare!" Agi grabbed my wrist. "We haven't eaten for days. You'll get sick and weak if you don't eat."

She didn't let go of me until I held my nose and poured the soup down my throat the way I used to take the medicine the doctor prescribed whenever I was sick back home.

We woke at dawn the next morning to the barking of the dogs and the curses of the Kapo.

Agi and I were on the top level of our three-tiered bunk sleeping with six strangers. We climbed down, our hands and feet full of pins and needles. We straightened our clothing as best we could. We weren't allowed to wash. Nor were we allowed to go to the latrines before we were driven outside. The Kapo's baton and the ss's truncheons and the threat of their boots hurried us along.

"Line up! Rows of five!" shouted the Kapo.

Agi and I stood side by side, droplets in a sea of prisoners. To my left was a small woman with a gentle face.

"My name is Eva Foldes," she said. "I am from Szombathely. I've been here for a month already."

I introduced myself. "Do you know where they took our parents? I want to find my mother and grandmother."

The woman seemed reluctant to reply. "I heard that the buildings with the chimneys . . . no, no. It's not worth repeating such nonsense."

"Please tell me what you heard! Not knowing is the worst of all."

"I was told that the people chosen to go left by Dr. Mengele after we got off the train –"

"Dr. Mengele?"

"He was the ss officer on the unloading ramp. He was the man who told us which way to go."

"He sent my mama and grandmama to the left. Where were they taken?"

She didn't answer for a long time, then pointed to the dark smoke belching from the tall chimneys behind us. "There is your family," she said so quietly that I had to strain to hear. "The Germans gassed them, then burned their bodies. The buildings with the chimneys are crematoria."

"I don't believe you!"

She hung her head. "It's true."

There was a sudden roaring in my ears. Spots appeared in front of my eyes. I opened my lips to scream, but Eva clamped her hand over my mouth.

"Don't be foolish!" she whispered. "If you call attention to yourself, they'll kill you!" She leaned over and caught hold of Agi's sleeve. "Your friend needs you!"

I felt myself slumping to the ground, but Agi and Eva grabbed my arms and held me up.

"They murdered our mamas and my grandmama!" My voice was a stranger's.

Agi's face blanched. "Dear God," she cried. "It can't be!"

"Agi, it must be true. Remember the bodies on the cart and what the man pushing it told us? Eva is saying they *gas* them and *burn* them." I was silenced by the bite of the Kapo's baton on my shoulders.

93

"Schweig, Jude!" It was the roar of a beast.

I stared past him, forcing myself to remain expressionless.

"So you think that you're better than me, Miss High-and-Mighty? You'll come off your throne soon enough!" the Kapo howled, marking each word with a blow of her baton to my head.

I bit my lip, determined not to let her see me cry, and tried to shield myself with my arms.

Fortunately, one of the ss called her and she left. Eva squeezed my hand.

"Take a deep breath. It helps with the pain."

The Kapo returned with the prisoner chosen by the ss to be the Blockälteste. The German officers themselves, the Kapo, and the Blockälteste marched between the rows and rows of exhausted and hungry women, counting and recounting the number of prisoners present. With each passing moment, the Kapo became more alarmed. Sweat poured from her brow. Her baton played feverishly on our shoulders.

We stood, hour after hour, prey to fear, absorbed in grief. Some women collapsed. Others were held up by their neighbors. My whole being was focused on staying on my feet. I couldn't even grieve for Mama and Grandmama, walking straight to their deaths. I concentrated all of my energy upon my own survival. Nothing else mattered.

There was a sudden shout from the block. "We found her!" Then gunfire.

We were dismissed.

"This can't be happening. It must be a nightmare!" Agi's voice was no more than a whisper. "We'll wake up tomorrow and it'll all be over."

13

Wednesday, July 5, 1944 — Wednesday, July 12, 1944

The nightmare did not end. We lined up again. This time it was for a breakfast of black coffee. We drank it squatting on the ground.

Agi made a face. "It's so bitter. It must have been brewed from weeds." But, like me, she drained her bowl. The tepid liquid soothed the hunger cramping my stomach.

The Kapo appeared. She separated the women in the block into groups of one hundred. I breathed a sigh of relief that Agi and Eva were with me. We were marched to the west end of the Lager. A huge pile of white bricks was piled beside the electric fence. The Kapo ordered us to move the bricks, two at a time, to the east end of the Lager, three or four hundred meters away. At first, I was quick and efficient, but as the summer sun rose in the sky, I became hot and thirsty. Sweat ran down my face and back. The bricks seemed to weigh more with each trip. My steps slowed until I was dragging myself across the void. I passed Agi and Eva. They were pale and moved heavily.

"I can't go on! I have to sit down," said Agi.

"If you sit, they'll shoot you!" cried Eva.

We toiled on. The summer sun was reaching its summit. I couldn't bear it any longer.

"I'll ask the Kapo's permission to get a drink," I told Eva.

"You can't! The water is infected. It'll make you sick," she said. "Courage. It's almost noon. We'll get soup. It'll quench your thirst."

The soup was lukewarm and watery and gave off a rancid odor, but it tasted better in my mouth than anything I had ever drunk before. After I drained my bowl, I was able to start working again.

The day seemed endless. The bricks in my arms became heavier and heavier, until I feared that their tremendous weight would make me sink into the ground and disappear. Silently, we trudged back and forth, back and forth, like clumsy beasts of burden, stumbling, dragging our feet. Mercifully, the sun went behind a gray cloud. I had a fanciful thought that it was hiding its shamed face. Hours later, the mountain of stone that had stood in the west end of the Lager stood in the east end.

Three hours of Appell, "lining up to be counted," followed, and I learned that I was stronger than I had thought possible. Sheer will power kept me on my feet. Then came dinner – a small piece of black bread and a tiny square of margarine. The bread tasted like sawdust. I was careful to bend down and pick up each and every crumb that dropped to the ground.

Finally, it was bedtime. One of the inmates showed me how to pick lice off my clothes and body. Agi and I examined each other carefully. No revolting critters were feasting on us.

"Nothing!" I crowed in relief.

"You mean 'not yet!' Give yourselves a few days. It can't be avoided. We are all infested." A cadaverous woman clomped over in wooden clogs like the ones Agi was wearing. She held out her hand. "Sari Lusztig," she said, "from Szombathely. Eva and I came on the same transport."

"I am Jutka Weltner from Pápa. We arrived two days ago."

"Ah! Newcomers to our resort! Enjoying yourselves?" she said. "You can't believe what you're seeing, can you? You tell yourselves that you're dreaming, don't you? Well, you're not! You are very much awake. The longer you're here, the more you will realize that this is a perverted world. Your worst nightmares have come to life. Believe the unbelievable!"

"Stop it, Sari! Stop it!" Eva had joined us. "You're frightening them. What's to be gained by that?"

Sari slunk off to her bunk.

The doors of the barracks flew open and the Blockälteste and the Kapo burst in.

"Blocksperre! Blocksperre!" they yelled.

"They're shutting down our block! None of us is allowed to leave the barracks, not even to go to the latrines," explained Eva.

"Why not?" asked Agi.

"I don't know," said Eva.

Soon we had the answer. The Czech family camp was located next to our Lager. We were forbidden from looking outside, but a terrible din filtered through the walls. Men and women were wailing, children were crying. We could hear people begging in Czech and in German. We listened to their suffering in silence. A Häftling asked the Kapo what was happening.

"They are going to the ovens!" She laughed. "Listen carefully! You might be next!"

Abruptly, the cries were replaced by singing. The lovely melody of the Czech national anthem and then of the "Hatikva" rose a thousand strong. Then the loud blast of truck engines revving up. The singing became fainter and fainter, until it could no longer be heard. I began to weep.

I had a dream that night – a dream I had had before. I was sitting in a sleigh pulled by beautiful white horses across a field of blinding snow. Mama and Grandmama were sitting beside me. Papa and Dezso were in the front, hanging on to the reins. Once again we passed the cowboy who tipped his hat and the Indian chief with the headdress the colors of the rainbow. Once again we came upon Miri, Klari, and Tamas, who were beckoning us to stop. Once again I saw tall buildings on the horizon. Once again an arm shook me back to wakefulness. This time, the arm belonged to Agi. It was time for Appell once again.

Appell was followed by breakfast. We were just finishing the acrid coffee when the Kapo appeared.

"It's time for you bitches to get back to work!" She swished her baton. With the aid of her German masters, she drove us back to the stone mountain. She pointed to the bricks, her beautiful face distorted. "You lazy good-for-nothings – move the bricks, two at a time, across the Lager to the west corner by the fence!"

"But yesterday we carried them here from that exact spot," said Agi. "It doesn't make sen –"

The Kapo's baton rang as it met Agi's head. She fell to her knees in the dirt.

"Idiot!" the Kapo roared. "Do you want to go to the ovens?"

"No, Kapo," Agi mumbled as the blood pouring from her nose mixed with the tears coursing down her face. She spat out a tooth and smeared her face as she tried to wipe herself clean with her sleeve. Eva and I helped her up.

"They make us work all day just to move a pile of bricks back and forth, for no reason at all . . . They are mad! And evil!" I said to Eva as we lined up for Appell again at the end of the day.

"You're learning quickly."

*

Day followed day. Up at five, hours of Appell followed by black coffee. Some days we cleaned the latrines, a long row of communal seats. Other days we lay around our bunk, doing nothing. I soon learned that any job was preferable to idleness. Work kept you from thinking. Lunch was a watery foul soup. Dusk was marked by hours and hours of Appell followed by a slice of dark bread and, occasionally, a small chunk of margarine. Then came restless, hot, overcrowded sleep, where the jerk of an elbow or the twitch of a foot resulted in bitter complaints from the person next to you. As I lay on the burlap mattress, wedged between Agi and Eva, I pleaded with God: *Please, God! Let me wake up in my own bed at home!* In the morning, as soon as I opened my eyes, I realized that God was not listening.

14

Thursday, July 13, 1944 — Monday, July 17, 1944

The tinny drumming of rain on the roof was keeping me awake. The room was black, except for a dim bulb above the entrance. Agi stirred beside me.

"You can't sleep either?"

"The rain," she whispered.

My stomach groaned. "Sorry. Can't help it."

"I'm hungry too," she said. "Do you ever think about lecso? All those peppers and onions. And an egg on top with a runny yellow yolk."

My mouth watered. "That's my favorite meal."

"Did your mama put a piece of sausage into her lecso? It gives it a nice, smokey taste," said a voice from the bunk directly below us.

"No, she didn't. We're kosher."

"We're kosher too," said a loud voice from another bunk below. "A wedge of kosher salami will give you the same flavor."

"My mama's lecso is so tasty that it doesn't need meat," I bragged.

"It's true," Agi said. "Her mama makes the best lecso in the world."

"What about cholent?" asked Eva. "Beans and barley, and onions and garlic . . . so yummy! My papa is a rabbi. We let it cook over Shabbos while we went to shul."

"Hush!" cried another woman before I could answer. "Some people are trying to sleep!"

I closed my eyes. I could taste the flavors in my mouth. During those terrible nights, I learned how to cook. The women loved to talk about their kitchens. As I listened, night after night, I remembered how Mama had shooed me out of the kitchen. "Two women in a kitchen is one too many!" she used to say. After the war, she'll let me help when she realizes that I know what I'm doing, I thought as I lay there half-dreaming. Then I would remember the tall chimneys, and I would cry myself to sleep.

On a hot July morning after our coffee ration, SS guards set up three long tables and rickety chairs in front of the barracks. At each of the tables sat two prisoners. One of them was clutching what looked like a medical instrument with a needle. His partner was in charge of a black ledger and a pen.

The Lagerälteste called for attention. "Each of you will be given a number!" he shouted. "Every woman will have this number tattooed on her arm. This number will be recorded. From now on, you will be known by this number. It will replace your name. Häftlings with surnames starting with the letters A to F, go to table one. Häftlings with names beginning with letters G to N, go to table two. The rest of you, go to table three. You disobey at your peril!"

Nobody spoke up.

"Haltet die Klappe!" bellowed the Kapo. "Line up! Single file!"

Long lines formed in front of each table. I headed toward the farthest one. The line moved slowly. There was only one person ahead of me when I felt a tug on my sleeve. It was Agi.

"Come with me!" she said.

"I can't! It's almost my –"

She leaned close. "Eva says that if our numbers are close together, we get to stay in the same block. Prisoners with higher or lower numbers may get moved to different blocks," she said. "If we want our numbers to be close together, we have to stay in the same line. Look at what this man's doing!" She pointed to the Häftling with the needle. I could see that he was tattooing large numbers on the forearm of the woman in front of me. "That woman," she said, pointing to the table with the longest line, "tattoos small numbers on the underside of your arm. Let's line up there."

"But my name starts with W."

"Don't tell them your real name – pretend your name starts with a letter from the beginning of the alphabet." She pulled my hand. "Come on. Eva is saving a spot for us."

I followed her. As we passed by the second table, we saw Sari at the back of the line. I motioned for her to follow us.

"What's the matter with you? Go back to your line before you get into trouble!"

When I told her what Agi had found out, she came with us. Nobody stopped us. Neither the Kapos nor the ss were paying attention.

Eva let us cut into the line in front of her at the first table. We waited for another hour. Finally, it was my turn.

"Your name?" the prisoner with the ledger asked.

"Judit Freis," I stammered.

He recorded my name in his book. Then the Häftling with the needle grabbed my arm. The pain was like a bolt of lightning. I clenched my teeth and stifled a scream. In a few minutes, it was mercifully over. On the underside of my forearm, neatly outlined in drops of blood and blue ink, was A10234.

15

Thursday, August 31, 1944 –
Friday, September 1, 1944

We lost everything – even our names. We had been reduced to numbers.

It was the end of August, and the days were cooler and constantly rainy. The Lager was full of mud. We had been moved to another miserable block, no better than the one we were in before. Agi, Eva, Sari, and I clung to one another as if we were the last people alive in a world of spirits. We spent the time wandering around the Lager or lying in our bunks. Our filthy uniforms hung loosely over our scarecrow frames. We were infested with lice.

The sun finally appeared. We had just received a scrap of bread and were squatting in the mud in front of the barracks eating.

"I thought the rain would never stop," said Eva as she

broke off tiny crumbs. She saw me watching her. "It lasts longer this way," she explained.

"I know. I do it too."

"So do I," Agi added.

Sari was leaning against the barracks wall, eyes closed, as if all the fight had gone out of her. She had become what the Häftlings called "Muselmann," somebody who had been broken by life in the camp and had lost the will to live. She was a walking skeleton with every rib showing, her skin gray, and her body and face covered with open sores. Over the last few weeks, she had become one of the living dead, but we pretended not to notice. She didn't take a bite of her bread.

"Why aren't you eating?" asked Eva. "Are you feeling sick?"

Sari's eyes remained closed, but a tear trickled down her cheek. "Do you know the date today?" she asked.

"I've lost track," said Agi.

"So have I."

"It's the end of August." replied Eva.

"It's my birthday," revealed Sari. "I'm nineteen years old today."

Agi gasped, and I understood why. The gray stubble on Sari's head, her toothpick limbs, her sunken eyes, and pale lips covered with sores – she looked like an old woman.

"Congratulations!" cheered Agi finally. "A happy birthday and many happy returns!"

Sari opened her eyes. "Congratulations? You must be joking! What do I have to celebrate? My mama and papa are gone," she said, waving her hand in the direction of the crematorium. Tears welled up in her eyes.

"We must be grateful that we're still alive," reassured Agi, putting an arm around Sari's shoulders.

"God will save us," added Eva calmly. "He will deliver us from the evil around us."

I kept quiet. My kind and gentle papa and Dezso, full of merriment. My darling mama and grandmama. All gone. For nothing, for nothing at all. I looked bleakly at the living hell around us, and no words came to my lips.

"We must celebrate your birthday somehow," said Agi. "Now what can we do? We have no food . . . nothing to give you."

Sari closed her eyes again "Don't bother – it's not worth it."

"Yes, it is!" cried Eva. "I remember how much we used to enjoy parties at home . . . oh the dancing, the music!"

Sari turned her head away.

That night, as I lay in the crowded bunk, Sari's face, so sad, so bereft of hope, swam in front of my eyes. I so much wanted to do something to lift her spirits, but what could I do?

The Kapo marched into the barracks as we were getting up the next morning.

"I need someone to help out in Kanada for the next few days," she hollered. "Any volunteers?"

Everybody's hand, except mine, shot up. I knew that the Kapo didn't like me. Why give her the satisfaction of passing me over?

We'd heard of the fabulous riches stored in the warehouses named after the country on the far side of the ocean, the land of my dreams. The Kanadians were the most fortunate among us. They were Häftlings who had been assigned to sort and store the possessions taken away from arrivals to Auschwitz-Birkenau. Sometimes the riches ended up in prisoners' pockets.

The Kapo scanned the room. "You all want to get away from here, don't you? Can't say I blame you!" She pointed her baton at me. "You are the only one who didn't volunteer. Are you too lazy to want to work, bitch?" she asked. "Come with me!"

I followed her outside to a jeep. She got into the driver's seat.

"Get in the back!" she snapped. "Lean away from me. I don't want to catch your lice!"

She revved the motor and we drove off. Her back was turned to me, offering a good view of her luxurious blond hair swept into a large chignon at the nape of her neck.

"What kind of work do you want me to do, Kapo?" I dared to ask.

She twisted her head in my direction. "Schweig!" she yelled. "Speak only when you're spoken to!"

I kept my eyes fixed on the floor of the jeep as if the antics of two busy lice crawling around on the top of my shoe fascinated me. The Kapo turned her attention back to her driving and sped up. A fat louse made its way up my leg. I picked it up and gently transferred it to the back of the

Kapo's uniform. She did not stir. I picked another louse from my sleeve and placed it carefully in the center of her chignon. Two more lice made their way to her back. She did not take her eyes off the road as she guided the jeep through the sea of dirty scepters listlessly moving along her path. Finally, we arrived at Kanada. As I stared at the large warehouses, I imagined for a moment fields of wheat and deep forests. But this Kanada was a series of warehouses, and I was staring at a mountain of clothing in front of one of them. I was handed over to one of the Kapos in charge of Kanada.

I stood at attention. He was the smallest man I had ever seen, under five feet tall, with a wizened face and a bulbous nose. His voice was very loud, as if he was trying to compensate for his diminutive size. I was relieved that he spoke in Hungarian. He led me into a large storeroom where coats of every color and size were piled high to the ceiling. He kicked aside a coat that had fallen from a pile to the floor before he spoke.

"Many of the Juden hide their treasures in their pockets when they are ordered to hand them over to the authorities before deportation," he said. I remembered the bracelet that Mama was forced to give to the gendarme at the fertilizer factory. "The Jews don't realize that their coats will be taken away from them at the end of their journey, so they stuff their pockets full with their money and their jewelry." He laughed heartily, as if he had just told a funny joke. He glanced around the warehouse. "There isn't much room here. Check the pocket of every coat for valuables. Move each coat over there," he ordered, pointing to the only empty corner in the room. "Put aside anything that you find for me. I'll be back!"

There was so much to do that I didn't know where to begin. Finally, I picked up a fashionable olive-green jacket. I imagined its stylish owner sitting in a café with other young women, gaily discussing her beaus as she ate sumptuous pastries and drank dark, rich espresso. The pockets of the coat were empty. Next came a man's elegant black overcoat. I could see its dashing owner bundled up in it, a black homburg on his head, as he walked to his law offices. The pockets of this coat were also empty. My pace was slowed down by images of the ghostly inhabitants of the clothing, but I felt I owed them the opportunity to tell their stories one last time.

I forced myself to concentrate on the pile of coats in front of me, for I knew that the Kapo would be returning, and he wouldn't be pleased to find me daydreaming. I looked in the pocket of every coat, but except for three handkerchiefs and a tube of lipstick, I found nothing. By the time the Kapo sent a Häftling with the message that I could have thirty minutes off for lunch, I had checked the pockets of more than half of the coats in the room. I was exhausted, and my shoulders and arms were aching.

It was definitely my lucky day. The prisoner dishing out soup from a large cauldron was a woman who had come to Auschwitz with my transport. When it was my turn to be served, I held out my dish: "Remember me from the train?"

She looked at me blankly at first, but then recognition dawned in her eyes. She dipped her ladle deep into the cauldron. The soup in my bowl was the thickest I had eaten since I'd arrived at the concentration camp. I sopped it up with a large piece of bread another Häftling had handed to me. I felt so full that I was afraid my stomach would burst.

I sat down on the ground to rest for a few minutes, leaning my head against the wall of one of the warehouses. The prisoners around me, who were mostly women, were well dressed and well nourished. Many of them were in civilian clothes, wearing white blouses with dark slacks. I was amazed to see that their hair was not shaved like mine. Häftlings in striped uniforms were clean and well groomed. Several of them asked for a second bowl of soup or another slice of bread. I was shocked to see that they were given food without beatings or curses. After a few minutes of rest, I was ready to return to the warehouse.

As the hours passed, I became more anxious. No matter how conscientiously I checked the pockets of the coats, I had nothing to show to the tiny Kapo. It was already midafternoon when I came across a woman's camel-hair coat with a beautiful fur collar – just like my mama's coat! I searched its pockets. They were empty. I stroked the fur and buried my face in its softness. It had the same smell as the perfume that Mama used to dab on her neck. I became more certain that I was holding my mother's coat in my hands. There was only one way to be sure. I examined the lining around the collar. As I ran my fingers over it, I felt a bulge. I heard Mama's voice, *Hurry, hurry!* I used my fingers to rip out the stitching that secured the lining to the material of the coat. It was hard going, because my nails were broken. I worked feverishly in case the Kapo returned to the warehouse. Finally, I had unpicked enough of the stitches to rip a hole in the lining. As I expected, several shiny gold coins were stitched against the material at regular intervals. Next, I loosened and removed the large cross-stitches that held the coins in place. I arranged the coins in a neat pile on the concrete floor.

I couldn't take my eyes off them. A dozen gold coins would let me organize a lot of extra bread. A dozen gold coins could mean the difference between life and death. There would even be enough money left over to pay for my train fare home when the war was over. I felt Mama's hand on my shoulder. I stuffed the coins into the pocket of my uniform. Then I put on Mama's coat, enveloping myself in her scent. For a moment, I felt as if she were a part of me. When I could delay no longer, I took off the coat and threw it on top of the pile of jackets I had already checked.

I got to work again. The heat in the warehouse was overwhelming, and I desperately wanted a drink. I was hot and tired and terribly frightened. I stopped sorting the coats and lowered myself to my haunches to think over the possibilities. I knew that the Kapo would be angry if I told him that I didn't find anything valuable. Would he even believe me? Would he not look in my pockets to make sure that I had not stolen anything? I ran to the entrance of the warehouse and poked my head outside. Still no sign of him. I emptied my pockets and piled up the coins on the floor, beside the handkerchiefs and the tube of lipstick.

As I worked, the money drew my eyes like a magnet. It occurred to me that even if the Kapo didn't believe that I had not found any valuables, he had no way of knowing what I actually did find. I was in an agony of indecision – sweaty and shaky from thirst and anxiety. Again, I poked my head out the door. There was still no sign of the Kapo, but I noticed a puddle of brackish-green water by the entrance. I couldn't resist it. I scooped up some of the liquid in my cupped palms and drank it down greedily. Then I hurried back into the warehouse, my mind made up. I picked up five of the coins. But where to hide them? If I didn't want them in my pocket, the only place to put them was in my shoes. I pulled down Mama's coat from the top of the pile and tore two long strips from the lining. Then I twirled the strips like bandages around my bare feet. I shoved the coins between the soles of my feet and the material. The coins dug into my skin, but I could still walk. I pushed the coat into the center of the pile, out of sight, and went back to work.

The Kapo didn't appear until the end of the day. He looked around the warehouse but didn't comment on the amount of work I had accomplished.

"Find anything?" he asked.

I pointed to the gold coins in the corner of the room. He picked them up, bit into them, and grunted in satisfaction before putting them in his pocket, together with the hand-kerchiefs and the lipstick.

"Turn your pockets inside out," he barked.

I did as he ordered.

"Lucky for you that you didn't try to pull a fast one! You're a good worker," he admitted begrudgingly. "I'll arrange for you to be permanently transferred to the Kanada detail."

I opened my mouth to thank him. I knew that in Kanada I had a chance to survive.

"That's very kind of you, sir, but I prefer to stay where I am," I heard myself say. "My friends are waiting for me."

The Kapo's face turned crimson.

"Don't you understand what I am offering you?"

I hung my head. "I am sorry, Kapo, but I prefer to stay in my Lager," I repeated. And I meant what I said.

"Get out of here!" he yelled. "Return to your block immediately!" He took an envelope out of his pocket. "Stop at the hospital on the way back and drop off a letter for me! Do you understand what I want you to do?"

"Jawohl, Kommandant!"

"Be gone!"

With a quick nod, I scurried out of Kanada, thankful that the Kapo did not think to check my shoes.

16

Friday, September 1, 1944

At the back entrance of the hospital, a tall man in a striped Häftling uniform came out of the building. He was bent under the weight of two pails hanging from his hands. He dumped the contents of the pails into a large wooden bin that stood at the side of the building. He jumped when I tapped him on the shoulder.

"Who are you? Why are you trying to sneak up on me? You're not supposed to be here!" He spoke so fast in German that I had difficulty understanding him.

"I was told to deliver this letter to the hospital."

He grabbed it and went back into the building.

My stomach growled, and I knew that if I didn't hurry I would miss my evening bread. The smell of food wafting out of the garbage bin made my mouth water. I looked around.

The road was deserted. I lifted up the lid of the bin. Resting on top of some soiled bandages was the large pile of raw potato peels the Häftling had dumped. I looked around again. Nobody in sight. I cupped my hands and scooped up some of the peels. They went straight into my mouth. I enjoyed every bite, and I ate until I couldn't eat another mouthful. Then I stuffed my pockets with as many of the potato peels as I could. I hurried back to the barracks with my stomach full, my pockets wet against my thighs, and the lumps made by the coins rubbing against the soles of my feet. I was happier than I had been since I arrived at Auschwitz. And I knew what I could do to help Sari celebrate her birthday.

Sari was lined up for bread with Agi and Eva.

"We were worried that you'd be too late to get your evening ration," said Agi.

"What happened to your skirt? Why is it wet?" asked Sari.

"I'll tell you after we've eaten."

It was finally our turn. With the precious pieces of bread we were given clutched in our hands, we sat down at our usual spot on the ground in front of our block. Agi and Eva gorged on their bread. Sari slowly nibbled on the crust.

"Happy birthday, Sari! I have a surprise for you," I said as cheerfully as I could. "They gave me extra bread in Kanada. I'm full. I can't take another bite. You can have my ration. It's my gift for your birthday." I shoved my bread into her hands before I could change my mind.

She stared at me, mouth agape. "I can't accept your bread! It's too generous!"

"Sure you can! You have to. I'm stuffed!"

Her face brightened. She hugged me and took the bread.

"There's more . . . I have something for you two!" I announced.

I emptied my pockets and filled my dish with the potato peels. The girls piled them on top of their bread.

"I am so hungry that it actually tastes good," said Eva.

"Let's be careful how much of it we eat," warned Agi. "We should save some for tomorrow."

"Don't worry about that. I can always organize more."

"Where did you get it?" asked Eva.

"It's better that you don't know."

Eva gave me a long look but did not press me.

"You are a good person, Jutka," said Sari, patting my hand, "giving me your bread, sharing the potato peels with us . . ."

"Nonsense! I was lucky. I told you, I was given extra bread in Kanada."

"Most people would have saved their ration for another day," said Sari.

Eva put her arm around Sari's shoulder. "Oh, how I wish that I had something to give you for your birthday too!"

"Don't be silly," said Sari. "We're in a Vernichtungslager. It's a death camp."

"Does that mean that you don't have a birthday? They're all the more precious here!" said Agi. "At my birthday parties, we always dressed up in our best clothes and stuffed ourselves with birthday cake and chestnut pudding."

She leaned closer to me. "You know, Jutka, both Sari and Eva have been here longer than us. Their clothes are in worse shape than ours."

"Thank you for pointing out that we're in rags." Eva struck a pose. "You're not so glamorous yourself!"

"Believe me, I know," said Agi. "Still, we're a little better off than you." She took Sari's hand. "Jutka and I will lend you our clothes to wear for a day, Sari. Jutka?"

"It's a wonderful idea!"

"You can have my shirt. It's less torn than yours – and much cleaner," said Agi.

Sari laughed helplessly. "Fine. But you really don't have to do this."

"I know, but I want to."

"Will your shirt fit me?" asked Sari.

"For sure. You may be taller than I am, but you're skinnier than me," Agi said.

"That's because you hardly eat!" I told her. "If you promise to eat more, I'll lend you my shoes." I kicked them off my feet.

"I am becoming a regular Muselmann, aren't I?" said Sari ruefully. She smoothed down the front of her tattered shirt.

"Don't be silly!" scolded Eva.

Sari sighed. "I know I am. Did you mean it about lending me your shoes, Jutka?"

"Of course I did!"

"I'd love to wear regular shoes, even if it's only for a day." She looked at my feet. "Why do you have rags wrapped around your feet?"

"Good question. Why?" asked Eva.

"Because I have another surprise!" I got the girls to stand in front of me so that I would be hidden. I unraveled the rags to reveal the gold coins. My friends stared at me.

"My God!" said Agi. "Where did you get them?"

"From Kanada. Don't ask any questions."

"But how –"

"Trust me, it's best not to know!" She nodded reluctantly, and I continued. "I want each of you to take a coin. The money will pay for your passage home at the end of the war."

"Or buy us bread so that we survive the war," said Eva.

"You should keep the money for yourself," said Agi. "You might need it."

"I have two coins. It's enough. I want to share the rest of the money with you." We decided that our pockets were the safest place for the coins. Nobody knew that we had them, so nobody would try to steal them from us. When the money was safely stowed away, Sari and I exchanged shoes.

"Your shoes are so comfortable!" she sighed. Her clogs felt tight against my toes, but I kept quiet.

Agi began to unbutton her blouse.

"Oh, Sari, I wish that I had something to lend you too!" said Eva. She looked down at her tattered dress. "I'm as shabby as you are." She scratched her head and flicked two fat lice into the air. Her face brightened. "That's it!"

she said. "I'll pick off all your lice. That'll be my gift to you!"

"The bugs will come right back," said Sari.

"They probably will, but they won't be so bad for a while," replied Eva. "Keep your shirt on for a little longer, Agi, until I debug Sari."

She picked off the lice crawling over Sari's body and clothes. She even captured the ones hiding in Agi's shirt before the two exchanged their clothing.

"You look nice," said Agi as we examined Sari in her borrowed finery.

Sari pulled herself up straighter. "I have the best friends in the whole world," she said. "How can I ever repay you? I promise to give back the shoes and the shirt tomorrow night." She turned to Eva. "And not to be itchy from lice – that is the best present!"

Our spirits were high when we returned to our block for the night. Agi and Eva slept next to me, but Sari slept in the last bunk on the far side of the room.

"I wouldn't have thought that it was possible, but I had a wonderful birthday today," Sari told us before she bade us goodnight.

A few minutes later, the front door of the barracks banged open and the Kapo entered. She was accompanied by an ss guard and a heavy-set man in an ss captain's uniform. I was glad to see the Kapo scratching her head.

"Attention!" She sounded nervous. "Disrobe completely, except for your shoes! Then I want everybody to line up beside their beds. Herr Doktor wants to have a look at you!"

"A selection! We're having a selection!" The message shot through the barracks as fast as a bullet. "They're going to kill us!"

"Silence!" thundered the Kapo. "There is no need for panic!"

The room became so quiet that I could hear my own pounding heart. The doctor marched between the rows of naked women standing at attention beside their bunks, the Kapo right on his heels. From time to time, he pointed his finger in someone's direction. The Kapo would escort the designated Häftling to join the others at the front of the room. The ss guard kept his rifle aimed at them.

I felt a tremendous rush of relief when the doctor walked by me. Nor did his finger move when he went by Eva and Agi. When he reached Sari, his finger pointed in her direction. In the blink of an eye, the Kapo led Sari to the doomed group waiting by the door. Sari passed by me, her face vacant. The ss soldier opened the front gate, and the women who had been chosen to be murdered were driven outside at gunpoint. Just before the door slammed closed behind her, Sari turned around.

"Your shoes," she cried. "Jutka, I forgot to return your shoes to you!"

I never saw her again.

That night I dreamt of Canada. Once again I was sitting in a sleigh pulled by beautiful white horses across a field of blinding snow, and everyone I loved was there. Then, suddenly, we arrived at a busy city, its tall buildings and crowded, snowy streets full of shiny cars. The streets teemed with smiling people, not a single uniform in sight.

"Canada!" I cried. "We have made it to Canada!"

The sleigh turned a corner, and Miri, Klari, and Tamas were waiting, shouting for us to stop. Papa pulled in his reins, and the sleigh came to a grinding halt. We scrambled down. Miri and Klari hugged me, and Tamas took my hand. He leaned forward and looked deep into my eyes. He was the old Tamas, with warm brown eyes and a gentle smile. My heart began to dance as I closed my eyes and waited for his kiss. The kiss did not come, and my eyes flew open. Tamas had disappeared. A tiger stood in his place. I stared into its yellow eyes and smelled its foul breath as it bared its fangs. I tried to run. I was breathing raggedly and was covered with sweat when the morning sirens woke me up.

Monday, September 18, 1944

I lost track of time. I did not know the day of the week or even which month we were enduring. Agi, Eva, and I found comfort from one another's physical presence. We talked of trivialities. We never talked about Sari, naked and terrified, led out of the barracks at gunpoint, or of the other lost ones. But their ghostly presence was always there. The days had become shorter and cooler, so I knew that fall must have arrived. The three of us were sitting in a corner of the block futilely trying to warm ourselves up with lukewarm coffee. Eva was unusually quiet.

"Eva? What's wrong?" asked Agi.

"Other than spending Rosh Hashanah in Auschwitz? What a way to mark the New Year!"

"How do you remember the date?" asked Agi.

"I count the days. It's Monday, September 18. When my papa was taken away, the last thing he told me was to mark the holy days."

"Think of all the lovely food we'd eat – the honey cake and raisins and soup with noodles. We won't be feasting this year," said Agi.

"And we won't be going to synagogue with our families," Eva added softly. "I would give anything to hear my papa's voice. He prayed so beautifully. I wish . . ." A single tear trailed down her cheek.

"Stop it, you two! It's useless to talk about what we don't have! At least we're together. The war can't last forever." I tried to infuse my words with a hope I did not feel. "'Who shall live and who shall die' – the answer's not in God's hands these days."

"You're right, Jutka," said Agi.

"My papa would be so disappointed in me if he knew that I didn't mark today," whispered Eva.

"There is nothing we can do," I told her.

"Yes there is!" Eva dragged herself to her feet and began to pray aloud. The Kapo rushed up to her.

"Silence!" she shouted. "Silence, or you'll pay for it!"

"No, Eva, no!" I cried.

"Eva, please," Agi pleaded. "Stop it!"

Eva ignored us. She turned her back on the Kapo and prayed.

When Agi saw that there was no stopping her, she stood up and added her voice to the recitation: "'Remember us for life, O King Who desires life, and inscribe us in the Book of Life, for Your sake, O Living God.'"

I couldn't help it. My legs seemed to have a will of their own. I stood too and clasped Eva's hand. Around us other Häftlings joined in, until all the women in the block were on their feet, hands linked as they chanted the words:

"'On Rosh Hashanah will be inscribed and on Yom Kippur will be sealed how many will pass from the earth, and how many will be created; who will live and who will die; who will die at his predestined time and who before his time . . .'"

Our voices rose: "'But repentance, prayer and charity remove the evil of the decree!'"

The Kapo marched up to Eva. "You'll regret you did this!" she screamed, spraying spittle into her face.

Eva stared back defiantly, without uttering a single word.

The doors slammed loudly shut behind the Kapo as she bolted out of the block. A few minutes later, she returned with two armed ss guards. Then there was a flash of fire, followed by thunder. Eva crumpled to the floor. We didn't even have time to say good-bye.

Two Häftlings dragged Eva's body away. Agi and I, wrapped in each other's arms, cried and cried, our tears intermingling, until we had no more tears left.

"First Sari and now Eva! I can't go on."

Agi clasped my hands in hers. "You have to, Jutka! Eva was so brave. She never forgot, not even for a moment, who she was. We must honor her memory by staying alive. I am going to fast on Yom Kippur because that's what she would have done!"

"So will I, for Eva's sake, although every day is Yom Kippur for us. But, Agi, I don't want to live in a world like this! Eva gone! Sari gone too! And our mamas and my grandmama! And where are our papas and my brother? I can't bear it!"

"You've also heard the rumors – the Germans are losing the war. We'll be free soon!" But her voice faltered.

"I doubt it! I . . ."

My words were cut off when the front doors of the barracks swung open. Two skeletal male figures in striped uniforms appeared, carrying a long table into the block. An armed SS guard followed them.

"They're men! Men!" The cry ran through the crowd of women who had not seen their fathers, husbands, and sons for months.

"Is there anybody here from Pápa?" the taller of the two prisoners called out.

"We are!"

Agi and I pushed to the front of the room. There was something familiar about the tall man. He was bald, gaunt, and filthy, but I was certain that I had seen him before.

Suddenly, Agi screamed.

"Jonah! Don't you recognize me? It's me! Agi!"

He stared at her, but there was no recognition in his face.

"It's me! Agi!"

A deep shudder ran through the man's frame, and he opened his arms wide.

"Oh my love, my beautiful girl! What have they done to you?" he cried. The barrel of the ss guard's rifle separated them.

"Raus! Raus!" cried the soldier, shoving him toward the door.

Jonah's friend followed the guard. "Come on, Jonah, come on!" he said. "Let's go before you get hurt!"

"I'm coming, Sandor," Jonah said. "I'm coming!" He stretched out his arms. "I love you, Agi!" he cried. "Don't forget me!"

"Do you know what happened to Papa?" Agi called after him.

"And to my father?" I asked. "Where is Dezso?"

"I was separated from them! I don't know where they are! I love you, Agi! Don't forget me!"

The guard pushed him out of the block.

18

Wednesday, December 27, 1944 — Friday, December 29, 1944

I had become a survival machine. My entire being was focused on staying alive. I was consumed with eating every last crumb of my daily bread ration. I even dreamt of running up to the steaming soup cauldron as it was brought into the Lager during lunch hour and dipping my spoon into it for an extra mouthful. I was always tired, but I refused to give in to the endless exhaustion that had crept into my bones.

October and November brought relentless rain. The Lager turned into a swamp. Our tattered clothes were caked with mud. Then came cruel December with its snow and icy winds, and our suffering deepened. We had no coats. Chilblains covered my hands. I dreamt of being warm. Selections occurred every few weeks. Hours and hours of Appell. Long waits in food lines. Our numbers dwindled.

One icy evening near the end of December, we were squatting on the earth floor, hunched over our bread rations. We huddled together for warmth. Our breath danced like ghosts as we spoke.

"I can't stand this much longer," said Agi. "I'm freezing. We need firewood."

The block was supposed to be warmed by hot air passing through chimney flues that ran through the building. The chimney flues were attached to a large brick fireplace in the middle of the block. However, we weren't given any fuel to build the fire that would have created heat.

"You can't be serious! There's no wood, and even if we had any to burn, we don't have matches," I said.

A mischievous grin appeared on her face. She reached into her pocket and pulled out two large wooden matches. "Surprise!"

"Agi, how did you get hold of matches?"

"The Blockälteste is quite fond of gold coins," she explained.

"You didn't! It was to pay your passage home!"

She shifted her position on the ground slowly, painfully, like an arthritic old woman. "Be reasonable, Jutka," she pleaded. "If we freeze to death, we won't have to worry about getting home. Right now, I just want to get warm. My joints are so stiff that I can hardly move."

"Give it up! Do I have to remind you again that we don't have wood?"

"I told you that I'll figure it out!" She looked so determined that I half believed her.

"It's not worth taking risks. You know what'll happen to you if you're caught!"

"I don't care," she said. "I can't go on like this any longer. I have to do something."

I was in bed after the lights were turned out, my teeth chattering with cold. I could feel Agi shivering as she lay next to me.

"I'm an icicle," she said.

I shifted to be closer to her. My leg touched a rough object lying between us on the mattress.

"What is—"

Her hand clamped over my mouth. "Hush!" she whispered. "It's a wooden plank."

I inched away from her for a better look. She had piled up several short wooden boards on the mattress.

"I've been pulling loose planks out of the bunks. They'll make perfect firewood. They're even the right length. I'll start a fire once everybody is asleep."

"Are you out of your mind? They'll kill you if they find out."

"I'll be careful. I can't bear being so cold."

I took a look at her – the wan cheeks, the pinched expression, the skeletal body with every rib outlined. She looked like Sari before she had been taken away.

"All right. If you're doing it, I'm helping." I hugged her.

"No! I won't hear of it."

"You're not doing it alone."

Her eyes filled with tears. "Thank you. Jutka, what's to become of us? Aren't they afraid that God will punish them for being so evil?"

Several hours must have passed because it was pitch-black when I felt Agi shaking my shoulders.

"It's time!"

She climbed down from the bunk carefully. I handed the boards to her one by one. Then I climbed down too, trying to make as little noise as possible. No one stirred as we carried the boards to the fireplace in the center of the room. We stacked the wood in it.

"Give me your matches! I'll light it."

"Oh no! I forgot to bring them. They're hidden in my shoes," she said. "I'll be right back!" She disappeared into the darkness.

I waited by the brick fireplace. It felt as if hours had passed, but it must have been only a few moments before she reappeared. It was so dark I couldn't see her face.

"What took you so long? Give me the matches!" I held my hand out in her direction.

The sudden light shining in my eyes blinded me. It was a few seconds before I could make out the Kapo.

"What do you think you're doing?" She was furious.

There was stirring in the bunk beds. Somebody turned on a light, and the Kapo lowered her flashlight. Behind her back, Agi was tiptoeing to our bunk.

"Where did you get the wood?"

I realized that I had to keep her attention focused on me. Agi had almost reached the bunk.

"What do you mean?"

"Don't play games with me, bitch! How did you get firewood? Where are the matches you were looking for? Who was helping you?"

Agi was hauling herself up the side of our bunk.

"I don't understand. I don't know what you're talking about," I said with as much defiance as I could muster.

She slapped me across the face. "Does that refresh your memory?"

Arms were reaching out of the bunk and pulling Agi up to the top level. I felt as if a tremendous load had been lifted off my shoulders.

The Kapo's attention was still fixed on me. "Talk, bitch! Where did you get the wood? Where are the matches?"

"I don't know!"

That earned me another slap.

"You're going to the Lagerführer's office! He'll improve your memory!"

I saw Agi sit up. Before she could speak, someone clamped a hand over her mouth and pulled her back down. My sigh of relief was so loud that I was afraid the Kapo would hear it.

"Scared, bitch? You should be!" Beating me with her baton and kicking me with her heavy boots, she drove me out of the block toward ss headquarters.

The blood flowing down my face tasted rusty. Every muscle, every bone in my body ached, but I knew I'd die before I gave the Kapo the satisfaction of hearing me cry. My silence enraged her.

"Scum!" she yelled, hitting me again.

We reached the headquarters as the winter sun was rising in the sky. I tried to focus on the pink sky, the very air around me, and even the pulsing of blood in my veins. Two armed guards informed us that the Herr Kommandant would be on duty in three hours' time. With a last blow of her baton, the Kapo left me.

I waited and waited, hour after hour, rooted to one spot in the corner of the room, afraid even to breathe, while the guards kept themselves occupied with steins of beer. I tried to keep my panic at bay by staring at a battered piano across the room and playing it in my imagination. My hands and fingers fell asleep, so I shifted my body.

"What's the matter with you?" called a guard. "Are you too impatient to wait for the Herr Kommandant? Would you prefer to go to the ovens instead? Things move more quickly there! That might be more to your liking!"

"Oh no, sir," I said. "I am not impatient at all. I am happy to wait for the Herr Kommandant. It's just the sight of the piano – would you like me to play for you?"

"Why not? It'll help pass the time."

I stumbled over to the piano. My fingers and feet tingled painfully as blood began to return to them.

"What would you like me to play?"

"Do you know 'Lili Marlene'?" asked the younger brute.

"Sure." I began to play.

Next came the German national anthem, "Deutschland über alles." I followed it with the marching songs that I had heard in the Lager. When I couldn't think of any more marches, I began to play every song I had ever learned. When I ran out of pieces to play, I began to improvise. The guards didn't seem to care as long as I kept the music fast and loud.

My arms and hands were aching, but I was afraid to stop. Through the barred windows, I could see the sun setting when another guard arrived to report that the Lagerführer would not be coming that day.

"What should we do with her?" the younger jailer asked.

"If the Herr Kommandant were here to decide – well, that would be different. I don't feel like bothering with her. It would mean extra paperwork. Let's get rid of her."

My pulse throbbed in my throat and spots floated in front of my eyes. I took a couple of deep breaths to calm down and forced myself to think logically. I still had the gold coins in my pocket. Should I bribe the guards with them? If they became angry, they could take the money away from me and kill me. If I didn't speak up, they would kill me for sure. I had nothing to lose.

"Respected Kommandants," I finally managed to squeak. "Please, please! I truly meant no wrong. To show you my good intentions, please accept a small gift." I reached into my pocket and handed each of the ss guards a shiny gold coin.

"Thieving Jew! Where did you get this money?" The older guard bit into his coin. "It's real gold."

"I want you to have them." The ss men looked at one another in indecision.

"What should we do, Erich?" the younger one asked.

"Let her go. That way, there won't be any explanations needed and no paperwork . . . and the money . . ." He patted his pocket.

The younger guard walked up to me and punched me in the stomach. I doubled over.

"Get out of here!" he snarled. "Get your hide out of my sight!"

I left before he could change his mind. I dragged my aching body back to the block. Agi was anxiously waiting for me. She cleaned my wounds as best she could. She had even saved half of her bread ration for my dinner. It was several days before I could move without pain.

19

Monday, January 8, 1945

We were the walking dead. Every day we heard rumors: "The Americans are about to bomb the crematoria! The Russians are getting closer!" But I had lost hope. Nothing changed, though our keepers were becoming more sadistic with each passing day.

The weather was frigid. Our thin clothing was no protection against the cold. The guards in their heavy overcoats, warm gloves, hats, and high boots devised a game. One afternoon, they divided my block into groups and ordered each group to run from one end of the Lager to the other. The men lined up along the running path, cheering us on. The stakes were high: life or death. An ss soldier caught the leg of any prisoner who was lagging behind and tripped her with the hooked end of his walking stick. As the poor Häftling lay on the icy road, another soldier took aim and shot her in the head.

Finally, it was our turn. I took off my wooden shoes and held them in my hands.

"What are you doing?" Agi asked. "Your feet will freeze!"

"The clogs slow me down. You should take yours off too!"

"It's too cold!"

A guard fired into the air.

"Rette sich wer Kann! Run for your lives!"

"Good luck!"

"You too, Agi!"

It took all my might and the good use of my elbows to propel myself through the crowd of jostling Häftlings. I dropped my shoes, but I kept going, straining for breath until I could see the finish line. I was a few steps away from it when there was a sudden cramp in my right leg. I stumbled, and crumpled to the ground. This can't be happening, I thought. But it was. I tried to get up, but the pain was so intense that I fell back into the snow. I heard laughter, and I found myself staring into the barrel of a gun. I was frozen, unable to move. Everything was happening in slow motion. The ss's finger moved toward the trigger of his rifle, but a sudden weight dropped on me, knocking the breath out of me and obscuring my line of vision. Then, a deafening bang. I lay stunned in the snow. I heard the sound of footsteps. They grew fainter and fainter until there was silence.

I wriggled, trying to get out from under the weight crush-ing me. I felt something roll off my body and was able to sit up. The ss were gone. Agi was lying face down on the ground beside me. Blood pouring out of her thigh stained the white snow. Her eyes were closed, and her breathing was shallow. She must have thrown herself on top of me and had taken the ss bullet instead.

I had to get help for her immediately. There was not a living person in sight, only the bodies lying by the road. I grabbed Agi under her arms and began to drag her in the direction of our block. It was slow-going, for the ground was rough, and I was so weak that I had to stop every few moments to catch my breath. My bare feet were numb. I was glad that Agi did not regain consciousness during the horrible journey.

Finally, we reached the first barracks. An inmate from Papa helped me put Agi into one of the bunks. Agi looked like a lifeless puppet as she lay on the dirty straw mattress.

20

Tuesday, January 9, 1945 — Friday, January 19, 1945

The camp was shrouded in darkness by the time I left Agi. I didn't have anywhere else to go, so I returned to my barracks. My feet were frozen, and I couldn't feel my toes. I stumbled over the body of a woman lying in the snow across the entrance. I crouched down and pulled off her shoes. They were too small, but they felt wonderful on my feet. My toes burned as they began to thaw.

At least a dozen women had died that morning. The rest of us were too dispirited to talk. Two or three were crying softly. Others lay mute on their bunks, staring into the air. I had trouble falling asleep that night, and when I did sleep I kept on reliving the nightmare. Over and over again I was staring into the barrel of the SS rifle. Over and over again

Agi was sacrificing herself for me. *Please, God, let my dear friend recover! Let her be whole again!*

The next morning there was Appell at dawn as usual. After, we were allowed to return to the block, I sat on my bunk and tried to think of a way to see Agi. I would have to bribe the Kapo, and I had nothing left to give her.

Suddenly, the door flew open and a dozen ss rushed in.

"Raus! Raus! Los! Los!"

We climbed down from our bunks, no questions asked. Before I left the barracks, I slipped the metal bowl that held my food in the daytime and served as a bedpan at night under my shirt. It was all I had left.

Outside, the other blocks in the Lager were also being evacuated. I became part of a long line of prisoners leaving Auschwitz-Birkenau. As we were herded past the barracks where I had left Agi, my eyes searched the crowd gathered in front of the building. She wasn't there. I tried to reassure myself that this meant nothing, that her wound was too fresh for her to get out of bed.

We marched out of Auschwitz, passing under a large sign declaring, ARBEIT MACHT FREI, Work Makes You Free. ss men with weapons and fierce dogs forced us westward on the icy road. Anyone who faltered or slipped lost their lives. After a while, I stopped wondering where they were taking us and focused all of my energies on keeping up with the others. It was so cold that I was afraid my lungs would burst.

When night fell, we stopped for a few hours in farmers' fields and rested on the frozen ground. We'd been walking for days when we finally arrived at a railway station. A locomotive was throbbing on the rails, with a long row of cattle cars attached to it. With their rifle butts, the SS shoved more than a hundred of us into each wagon. There was no room to move, barely enough air to breathe. The doors shut, and the train pulled out of the station.

"We won't be here long," I heard someone say. "The Americans will be coming soon!"

"The Nazis are going to exchange us for the German prisoners of war who were captured by the Americans," said another Häftling.

The train kept going. We had no water to drink or food to eat. There were no windows, so it was hard to know when the day ended and the night began.

Finally, the train stopped for a while, but the doors of the wagon remained closed. We were too weak to talk. I kept drifting off into jumbled dreams. I saw Agi lying on the icy snow with the SS rifle pointed at her head. Then I was traveling in a sleigh pulled by white horses galloping toward a city of bright spires. I was back in Kanada jumping for joy as I found the gold coins in the lining of Mama's coat. Suddenly, the buzzing noise of airplanes overhead woke me. There was loud banging outside.

"The Americans must be bombing the train!" somebody cried.

Then there was a scraping noise, and the doors of the cattle car slid open. Two Polish prisoners dressed in bedraggled striped pajamas stood at the entrance. A Häftling translated what they were saying.

"The Americans bombed the train!" they cried. "Our wagon was hit and caught fire. We managed to break down the door. Run for your lives!"

The cold air streaming into the cattle car revived me. I struggled to my feet and followed the others to the open door.

The platform was filling up with prisoners. Two or three SS, their heads bent, walked by us without raising their eyes.

"Do you know where we are?" I asked an emaciated Häftling.

"I have no idea," he replied in Hungarian, "but we must be somewhere in Austria or Germany." He pointed to the German signs on the station wall.

Something about the prisoner seemed familiar. I looked at him more closely. He was the man who had helped Jonah bring a table into the barracks, a million years ago, it seemed.

"You are Jonah Goldberg's friend, aren't you?" I asked.

He laughed. "I plead guilty." He extended a bony hand. "I am Sandor."

"My name is Jutka. I am Agi's friend."

"Where is Agi? Is she with you?"

I explained to him how Agi had saved my life. "I don't know if she'll recover."

"You must hope for the best," he said. "I was separated from Jonah during the march. I hope he is all right."

An unarmed ss passed us silently, his eyes fixed on the ground.

"What's the matter with them?"

Sandor laughed again, and I realized that beneath the grime covering his face he was still a young man, only a few years older than me. Blond stubble covered his head, and the knowing look in his piercing blue eyes was far beyond his years. He turned to one of the ss.

"Hey! What's going on?"

"We heard the war might be over," the ss mumbled, "but we're not sure."

Someone shouted for joy.

"Let's be careful," warned Sandor. "We don't know what's going on."

"Look at them!" An older Häftling pointed at the silent ss. He spat on the ground. "The war must be over!"

"We don't know for sure," repeated Sandor. "Let's wait before we do anything."

"You're too cautious, Sandor," said the older man.

Sandor grinned. "I am not impulsive like you, that's for sure."

"Let's get them!" cried another Häftling.

The ss men broke into a run with a group of prisoners in pursuit. Sandor grabbed my hand. "Let's go!"

We ran into the station house. It was deserted. Dust motes danced over an empty desk covered by an open ledger.

On one side of the ledger stood a bottle of ink with a pen dipped into it. There was a cup of coffee on the other side of it. I picked up the cup. It felt warm under my fingers, so I drank half of it. It took all of my willpower to give Sandor his share.

We went into the bathroom. There was not a soul in sight.

"Real toilets!" said Sandor. "What luxury!"

I washed my hands, marveling at the warm water, and glanced in the mirror hanging above the chipped sink. The gaunt, grimy, bald stranger with hollow eyes staring back at me was frightening.

"Stop primping!" joked Sandor. "We have to get out of here."

We crossed the empty field behind the station house and found a village, consisting of a church and a dozen dilapidated houses, built around a central square covered with dirty snow. We did not see a single person.

We knocked at the first house and rattled the lock, but the door remained closed. The door of the second house gave way under the weight of our shoulders. We searched the entire house, calling for the owners, but nobody answered until I noticed the tip of a boot sticking out from underneath one of the beds. Sandor grabbed hold of it and out came a farmer. His wife crawled out behind him. She shrank close to her husband, holding on to his arm. The couple stared at us with eyes filled with loathing and fear.

"What can you give us to eat?" barked Sandor in German.

"We have nothing except some milk and bacon," said the old lady.

"I can't eat bacon," I whispered in Sandor's ear. "I have never eaten pork."

"That was then," said Sandor.

"Give us whatever you have," he said to the farmer and his wife.

The woman scurried into the kitchen, reappearing with an earthenware pitcher and a slab of bacon. She pushed the food into our hands.

Sandor poured the milk into two tankards and cut two generous slices from the bacon. We sat down at the table and motioned to the man and his wife to join us. They remained standing, their faces full of resentment.

My hands trembled so badly that I spilled the milk down the front of my uniform. I couldn't taste the bacon as I jammed it into my mouth.

"Slowly," warned Sandor, "you must eat slowly, or you'll be sick."

When we were finished, Sandor divided the remainder of the slab of bacon in half. He tied his own portion around his waist with a string the man gave him. I put my share into the metal bowl in my shirt and tucked it away again.

A loud shot cracked outside. I grabbed Sandor's arm.

"They've found us!"

"Don't worry," he said. "One of the Polish boys must be

evening the score. Let's see what's going on." We stepped outside.

"Get down on the ground, Jews!" an angry voice shouted as soon as the door closed behind us. It was the Volkssturm, the local volunteer militia. We lay on our stomachs in the snow with at least two dozen other Häftlings, surrounded by a mob of armed farmers, their weapons pointed at our heads. One of the Volkssturm shot his rifle into the air.

A few minutes passed. The farmers seemed to be having a muted but furious argument.

Finally, their leader growled, "Get up!"

We struggled to our feet.

"Go!" He waved his rifle in the direction of a small forest behind the church.

Sandor grabbed my arm. "No! If we go to the forest with them, they'll kill us!"

The Häftlings took up the cry: "Not the forest! Not the forest!"

"Have it your way!" The leader of the farmers spat on the ground. "Back to the train with you!"

The armed men herded us at a trot in the direction of the cattle cars. When we got to the railway station, the ss were waiting, lined up in a single row in front of the station house. They fired their rifles at us.

"Dear God, what should we do, Sandor?"

"Run as close to the line as you can! If you're close enough, they won't be able to shoot you."

147

It took all of my courage to run right in front of the line of ss men and their rifles. I prayed, "Hear, O Israel, the Lord our God, the Lord is One." I thought I was about to die. Something banged into me with great force, knocking me sideways. It felt as if I had been struck by lightning. The ss man closest to me had a bloody bayonet in his hand. He laughed in my face.

"You want freedom, bitch, I'll give you freedom!" he yelled.

I woke up in the dark, struggling to breathe. I was wedged between two cold masses. I pushed and pushed until I was finally able to crawl forward. My back was throbbing. Suddenly, I felt fresh air on my face, and I rolled down a bumpy hill. I lay on the snow, panting. When the full moon emerged from behind a cloud, I realized that I had just crawled out of the center of a mountain of corpses. I began to retch.

When I could breathe more calmly, I washed my face with snow. I heard a faint sound in the distance. I tried to get up, but the pain in my back was so intense that I couldn't stand. I began to crawl in the direction of the sound. The noise grew louder and louder. I could hear people speaking and was finally able to see the cattle cars on the railway track. When I reached the first wagon, a hand reached down from the opening and pulled me up. I fainted.

21

friday, January 19, 1945 — Thursday, february 15, 1945

Sandor's blue eyes were the first thing I saw when I regained consciousness.

"Welcome back," he said. "I was afraid I had lost you."

"Oh, I'm not that easy to get rid of!"

I realized I was cradled in his arms, and I started to feel self-conscious. I was filthy and I reeked. I drew away from him, sat up, and flexed my legs and arms. Everything seemed to be in working order, but the left side of my body and my entire back was throbbing. A large dressing made of a piece of uniform had been wrapped around my waist.

"What is this?"

"You were bleeding," said Sandor. "The metal dish you had tucked under your shirt saved your life." He picked up the bowl I had brought with me from Auschwitz. "See how deeply it's dented? It deflected the bayonet. You should heal in a few days."

That's when I noticed that his striped pajamas were missing a sleeve.

He looked around the wagon furtively, and when he saw that nobody was listening, he said, "I filled up my dish with snow before the train left and saved you some of the water." He held his bowl to my lips. "Slowly," he said, "drink slowly."

I drank down the tepid liquid, then ate what was left of the bacon. There were a lot fewer of us than before. Only a handful of Häftlings were stretched out on the wagon floor. The rest must have died or run away.

"Where are we going?" I asked.

"I have no idea, but we've been traveling for three or four days. We haven't been given water or food. I felt mean not sharing my rations, but I wanted to save them for you. Lean on me and rest."

I did as I was told and fell asleep immediately. When I awoke the next morning, I felt stronger. However, with each passing hour, I became more and more thirsty. It was a tremendous relief when the train came to a stop.

We climbed out of the wagon and found ourselves in a bustling railway station. Long lines of trains were coming and going despite the late hour. Damaged locomotives and passenger cars lay overturned on the tracks. Armed SS were everywhere.

"The station has been bombed," said Sandor.

A sign by the station house read, MAUTHAUSEN.

"Be careful," he said. "I've heard about this place. It's a Vernichtungslager. There are ovens here."

An ss soldier approached our group: "Schweig! Men on the left! Women on the right!"

"Don't tell them that you're injured," said Sandor.

I squeezed his arm in farewell, and he was gone.

They made us climb a steep hill, where we lined up for registration that seemed to last forever. I was so focused on staying upright so that I'd look strong and energetic that I barely noticed the Häftling who collapsed beside me.

We were given a bowl of watery soup. Despite my raging thirst, I forced myself to drink slowly.

Next, we were put into quarantine in a large, empty barracks with wooden floors. Each of us was given a rough blanket from a pile in a corner of the room. We lay down on the floor until every centimeter was covered by our bodies.

The days that followed were sadly familiar – Appell, brutality, starvation, and misery until we were moved into yet another Lager.

I spent the days sitting on the ground in a corner. My thoughts were more real to me than the wretchedness surrounding me. My mind wandered, and at times I would find myself in Canada, dressed in furs, riding a glossy, black horse while Agi rode on a white horse. Mama and Grandmama, in their warm winter coats, stood by the side of the road, waving to us. Papa and Dezso were there. Klari, Miri, and Tamas gathered on the other side of the road. The horses vanished, and I was driving in a luxurious car through streets lined with tall buildings and bustling with happy people in summer clothes. Agi kept repeating, "Everything is much nicer in real life than in the pictures in your Canada book!"

Then I would find myself back in the Lager and would begin to weep. Only the thought of Sandor gave me a vestige of hope. In the middle of February, I saw him again.

The Americans had begun to bomb the Mauthausen railway station, and we were taken there to repair the damage. We cleared debris from the tracks while male Häftlings from another Lager turned the train cars upright.

I was so weak that all of my attention was focused on the task before me. I was filling my arms with rocks when someone tapped me on the shoulder. I dropped my load, and I fixed my eyes on the ground. Not only was I too tired to lift my head, I also wanted to spare myself the sight of the grinning face of an ss soldier before he struck me down.

"Have you forgotten me already?"

My heart jumped. It was Sandor – an even more skeletal, more bedraggled Sandor, with one of his front teeth missing, but a Sandor whose blue eyes were burning as brightly as ever despite his grimy face. I laughed and cried at the same time. We embraced before a truncheon could part us. Sandor picked up a few rocks. I helped him clear the tracks.

"Are you all right?" he asked.

All of a sudden, the misery filling my heart poured out of my mouth the way water escapes an overturned bottle. I began to cry.

"I can't go on! Everyone I ever loved is gone! This hell will last forever!"

Sandor dropped the rocks and took my face between his hands. By some miracle, none of the SS guards was looking in our direction.

"You can't give up!" he said. "The Americans are getting closer every day. They bombed this station! I heard that the Soviet prisoners of war scaled the walls of the Lager and escaped. Some of them got away!

"Be strong! Look, I need you. I don't have anyone either," he whispered. "They made us work in the quarry and in the tunnels. We are less than animals in their eyes. The thought of seeing you kept me going," he said shyly.

He let go of me and melted into the crowd as an SS soldier came toward us. I went the opposite way.

In the evening when we trudged up the hill, I searched the crowd, but I could not see him anywhere.

22

Tuesday, April 10, 1945 —
Saturday, May 5, 1945

On a sunny, mild April morning, we were ordered to go to the tents set up outside the walls of Mauthausen.

Fourteen of the largest tents I had ever seen had been erected. They were so crowded with newly arrived Hungarian Jews that there was barely any room to move. Many were sick or dying. They'd been allowed to keep some of their belongings. I saw people sleeping on their monogrammed sheets and pillows spread out on the muddy ground. Häftlings who could not find space inside the tents slept in the dirt outside.

I felt totally alone in that mass of people. It seemed that it was me who had vanished, not those I loved. But there was a chance that Sandor was still alive, and I set out to find him. Nobody recognized his name.

"He is probably dead," cackled an old man. "All of us will be dead soon."

I put my hands over my ears, but his words followed me.

The hunger was worse than in the camp up the hill. Rations were cut back. By the time the order came for us to evacuate the tent camp, I was so weak I could barely stand. I didn't know where we were heading, and it didn't matter. I had learned by then that hell has many chambers.

We were forced to march at a relentless pace. Faltering meant a Nazi bullet. In a strange way, we became invisible. As our spectral crew staggered through the bombed streets of Linz and Wels, the townspeople seemed oblivious to our presence. The streets were full of life. Mothers pushed their babies in prams among the ruins. Shopkeepers were serving their customers. Children were riding their bicycles. But no one seemed to notice the living skeletons in their midst.

We were desperate for food and water. One night, we were given a short rest in a farmer's field. I was lucky. I found two withered potatoes. I shared them with two women. We crammed grass and weeds into our mouths. "The salad course," said one of them. Another time, we had an hour's rest by a river and drank greedily from the turgid waters. We caught snails and ate them. Anything to feed our bellies.

Finally, near Gunskirchen we dragged ourselves up the side of a hill, on top of which, in the bush, another camp had been built. We staggered through the gates. The camp was what I'd grown to expect – filthy barracks, masses of emaciated people, and bodies everywhere. I closed my eyes for a second to make my surroundings disappear. When I opened them again, Sandor was coming toward me.

It was the day of my fifteenth birthday when the news spread through the camp that the International Red Cross had sent us packages. Even more incredible, our brutal guards were letting us keep them. Sandor and I were sitting under a tree, opening our parcels. They contained riches: food I had not seen for an eternity – chocolates, salami, crackers, even powdered milk. We ate and ate. Then we lay down on the grass, our bellies full.

"I haven't eaten so much since we left home," I groaned. "It's a nice way to celebrate my birthday."

Sandor rolled onto his side to face me. "Happy birthday!" he said. He pulled me close to him and kissed me. I was astonished. My first kiss! And then I kissed him back. I forgot the camp, the lice, and the tall chimneys of Auschwitz. I forgot everything except the warmth of his lips and the blood coursing through my veins. I gently pulled away from him.

"All this talk of birthdays makes me homesick," I stammered. I was too shy to meet his eyes, so I busied myself with plucking handfuls of grass from the ground. "Do you think that we'll ever be able to go home? I want to be with my father and my brother. I'm praying that Agi will make it home too."

Sandor sat up. "When I saw my parents and my sister head toward the gas chambers, I knew my home was gone.

I'm going to Eretz Israel when the war is over. I'll never be a stranger again."

We watched two Häftlings stumble under the weight of a cauldron of soup they were carrying into the yard.

"I don't want soup," said Sandor. "I'm too full."

"So am I, but I am thirsty. The soup will help." I was not about to turn down any food.

I got up and joined the line. A Häftling filled my bowl up to the brim.

"Why so generous?" I asked. Usually, we were lucky to have our bowls half filled.

"Orders of the Kapo . . . don't ask me why."

I carried my bowl back to Sandor and sat down on the grass beside him. The first mouthful stopped me short. I spat it out.

"It tastes horrible! It's sweet!"

"Let me try some," said Sandor.

"Something has been put into this soup! It's not safe to drink it." He poured it out.

He was right. Within hours, the prisoners who had finished their portion of the soup became violently ill. Many of them died.

One afternoon, without any warning, the guards ran away.

The cry went up: "The war is over!"

I rushed to the kitchen. Prisoners were at one another's throats, scrambling for bread. Over the din, I heard my name: "Jutka!" It was Sandor. "It's too dangerous to stay here! Let's go!"

In the first few hours of freedom, I felt nothing except a bone-deep weariness. Then I began to think about everyone I had lost: Mama and Grandmama walking to the crematorium; Agi lying in the snow, a bullet in her thigh; Papa and Dezso waving good-bye at the railway station. All was suffering and death and chaos. And all for nothing! For nothing! I was afraid to think of what the future would bring.

We slept on the hillside outside of the camp gates that night. The brightness of the spring sun woke me up the next morning. Suddenly, a man jumped to his feet.

"The Americans are here! The Americans are here!" he cried, pointing to the highway at the bottom of the hill. A long line of tanks and jeeps was making its way down the road. We scrambled down the hill to meet them.

"The Americans are here! The Americans are here! Help us! Help us!"

I almost ran into a tank at the bottom of the hill. The driver came to a stop. He was a large GI with shiny black skin, and he was munching on a sandwich. He stared at me, his mouth open, his sandwich in midair. He leaned down and held it out to me.

"Take it!" he said.

In that moment, I knew we were saved.

III

Paradiso

23

Sunday, May 6, 1945 — Saturday, June 30, 1945

When I was a little girl, my parents gave me a canary for my birthday. I thought that it was the most beautiful bird I had ever seen. I stood in front of its cage every day, listening to it sing. Once, when Mama left the room, I decided to set it free. As soon as I unlatched the cage, it flapped its wings and hopped to the open door. Then it stopped. It didn't fly into the room. It stood trembling, and then covered its head with its wings. When Mama came back, I asked her why the bird hadn't flown away. She said that it stayed in its cage because it had nowhere else to go.

The door of our cage was open. I felt so weary, so confused, and so empty that it took time before I could believe that there would be a tomorrow.

When Sandor made a bad joke – "I am sick and tired of living in camps" – I laughed.

"I'm leaving," he said. "I want to live like normal people, even if it's just for an hour. Let's go into Linz."

"We have no money, no papers."

"But I have a plan." He grinned and grabbed my hand. "Come with me!"

"I can't. I want to start for home. Papa and Dezso are there."

"You don't know that. If they went through what we went through . . ." He didn't have to finish his sentence.

"I feel it in my heart that they must be all right," I said. "Wouldn't I feel it if they were dead?"

"I guess you have to find out for yourself," said Sandor quietly. "For now, come with me. I intend to get food and some decent clothes. Then, back to Pápa . . . I'll go with you. The roads aren't safe for a young woman by herself."

"You don't have to do that!"

He put his arm around my shoulders. "Yes, I do. I want you to be safe. Besides, I have no place to go until I can get to Eretz Israel."

The road to Linz was thick with army jeeps, tanks, cars, carts drawn by skeletal horses, and people traveling on their own two feet. It was slow-going, especially when we came upon the carcasses of starved horses. As soon as a horse went down, it was surrounded by a ravenous throng.

The crowd had thinned by the time we got to Linz. We turned down a side street. It was lined with apartment buildings, many of them bombed to ruin. Women and old men were sifting through the rubble. I could feel their hostility as they took in our prisoner garb.

The last apartment house on the street was standing intact. Two American soldiers came down the gray steps. One of them was carrying a large cake decorated with white icing. The other had a cigarette dangling from his mouth and a jug of wine tucked under his arm.

I wanted that cake fiercely. My fifteenth birthday had just passed – this cake was for me! I grabbed it and ran. Sandor followed, with the soldiers close behind. We were no match for the Americans. They caught up with us without any trouble. I thrust the cake back into the soldier's hands, ashamed.

"Here, take it!" I spoke in German as I tried to catch my breath. "I am sorry. I don't know what possessed me. It was my birthday yesterday and your cake . . ." I sobbed.

"Take it easy," said the GI. "I'm not mad."

The second GI threw down his half-smoked cigarette and ground it out with his heel. I was debating with myself whether I should pick it up when Sandor stooped down and put it into his pocket.

He said to the American, "This stub will buy us a loaf of bread."

The GI laughed.

"Consider it a gift. Buy something with it for your girl-friend."

"How old are you, girl?" the soldier with the cake asked.

"Fifteen, sir."

An expression I could not identify flitted over the soldiers' faces. The soldier handed the cake back to me.

"Enjoy it! Happy birthday!"

His friend thrust the jug of wine into Sandor's hands.

"Have a drink to celebrate!" he said.

They bid us a cheerful good-bye and were gone. We called after them as they made their way down the street, but they just waved back before turning the corner.

"Well," Sandor said, "we have our supper, but we need a table. I want to sit in a chair at a table."

A week earlier, I would have stuffed handfuls of cake into my mouth wherever I happened to be standing. But now Sandor's words made sense.

I followed him up the steps of the apartment house. My head was aching.

"What are we doing here?"

"I don't know yet," said Sandor. "I just want to eat a piece of cake like a civilized person."

We were in a marble foyer with corridors at both ends. We chose the hallway on the left and rang all the doorbells. Nobody answered. Then we tried the corridor on the right. All of the doors remained closed.

"Let's get out of here and go back to the camp. My head is pounding."

"Come on," he said. "Somebody must be home. Let's try the second floor. If nobody answers, we'll go back."

We climbed the worn marble steps and began ringing doorbells. The building was either deserted or everybody was afraid to answer their door.

"Let's go back to the camp," I said. I couldn't think of anywhere else to go.

"One more apartment." Sandor rang the doorbell of the apartment at the end of the hall. A small, gold nameplate read, FRANZ AND GERDA SCHMIDT.

We heard footsteps and the door swung open. A middle-aged man, wearing the Austrian ss uniform, was pointing a pistol at Sandor's head. His wife was standing behind him, crying and wringing her hands.

"What do you want, dirty Jew?" The man waved his pistol.

Sandor pulled himself up, dignified in his filthy, drooping stripes. "I'm sorry now that we came to warn you to get out of your apartment before the mob of Jews gets here. They're going from building to building looking for Nazis. They have knives. As soon as they see your uniform, they'll string you up."

"He's lying!" said Schmidt to his trembling wife.

"Have it your way." Sandor turned to me. "See, Jutka, I told you that you're too softhearted. We should have let the boys have their fun with them. We only came to warn you, because my girlfriend does not want to see more bloodshed."

"Franz, I beg you, listen to them!" The man's wife was frantic. "Let's leave while we can."

"Schweig, Gerda! Let me think." He lowered his gun. "All right, let's get out of here! Hurry!" he yelled at his wife. She grabbed her coat and hat. "We're going, but we'll be back. We are going straight to the Americans. They'll protect us from the likes of you."

As soon as they were gone, Sandor pulled me inside and shut the door behind us. I put the cake on the hall table.

"That wasn't too bad," he said.

"But, Sandor, we'll get into trouble when the Americans find out that we lied."

He laughed. "The Americans won't care. We'll give back the apartment, but we'll have soft beds to sleep in tonight." He grabbed my wrist. "Come on, Jutka. Let's look around."

The water was lukewarm, but I giggled with pleasure as it tickled my body. I ran my fingers over my legs. Looking at myself was like looking at a stranger. My skin was gray and my nails were blackened. I could count every rib. I splashed water over my arms, covered with sores I had picked raw. Then I leaned back and closed my eyes.

I didn't want to get out of the cool water, even though the smell of frying eggs made my stomach growl. I climbed out of the tub and dried myself with one of Frau Schmidt's thick towels. I didn't have a toothbrush, so I rubbed my teeth with the side of my fingers. Then I wrapped a towel around my body and found the bedroom.

I stood in front of Frau Schmidt's massive mahogany wardrobe. It seemed vital to pick the right dress. I finally settled on a pretty blue cotton frock with a pattern of pink flowers. It was enormous on me, but it had a sash that I twisted around my waist twice. The Frau's feet were much smaller than mine, so I had to make do with my battered camp shoes. I wiped them clean and borrowed a pair of stockings from the wardrobe. I finished by wrapping a pink silk scarf around my shorn head. When I was dressed, I twirled in front of a long mirror. Although the girl looking back at me was much thinner and had huge, hollow eyes, she reminded me of the Jutka I had seen in the mirror of my dresser back home.

Sandor was in the dining room. He stood up when he saw me and led me to the table. The room looked romantic. He had drawn the curtains against the twilight. A candle flickering in the middle of the table was the sole source of light. He had set the table with Frau Schmidt's china. In addition to the eggs he had fried, he had toasted slices of dark bread. The cake, icing smeared, sat on a crystal plate. The bottle of wine stood next to the candle.

We sat down at the table wordlessly. Sandor was wearing one of Schmidt's suits. He had washed in the kitchen, and the stubble on his head was still damp.

"You look pretty, Jutka."

"You look nice yourself."

He ladled eggs onto my plate, and we began to eat. I picked at my food, even though the eggs were delicious. My headache was getting worse.

"Is there something wrong?" he asked.

"I guess I'm not hungry. I have a pounding headache."

He put his fork down. "That's enough for me too. We'll leave the cake. Go and rest. I'll clear the dishes away."

I sat down on the couch in the parlor and waited while he piled the dishes into the kitchen sink. I closed my eyes, praying that my headache would go away.

"Well, that didn't take long," said Sandor, sitting down beside me. He put his arm around me, and I rested my aching head on his shoulder.

I snuggled close to him as if I could draw some of his strength and vitality into me.

We sat in silence in the stuffy parlor of two Austrian strangers, and for the first time in a long time, the old Jutka came back to me. A wave of homesickness swept over me, so strong that it made me feel faint. I wanted everything to be the way it was before the war.

"Your plan's working, Sandor," I said. "Isn't it amazing? A bath and clean clothes made me feel like myself again. But I am still confused. Here I am, sitting on a brocade couch, the same person who ate garbage and was happy to get it. I don't understand anything anymore. Nothing. All I know is I have to go home."

"I know, Jutka, but give yourself a few more days to get your strength back." He held my face between his hands and kissed the tip of my nose. "I meant it when I said that I'd go with you. I want to keep you safe." He stood up and took my hands. "Your hands are hot."

"I am just tired."

He yawned. "So am I. It's getting late. Let's get some sleep."

I followed him to the bedroom, as if in a trance. Then we heard a key rattle in the lock.

"Damn!" Sandor was close to tears. "I didn't think that they'd be back so soon!"

Schmidt and his wife stomped into the apartment, accompanied by two American military policemen.

"What will they do to us?" All the panic of the last months seized me again.

I stepped forward, swayed, and crumpled to the floor at their feet.

24

Tuesday, July 3, 1945 —
Tuesday, July 31, 1945

The fever dreams trapped me. I was back in Kanada, sorting through mountains of coats. Then I was lying in my bed in the ghetto, until Klari and Miri shook me back to wakefulness. I opened my eyes and found myself sitting in a large sleigh. I was dressed in my school uniform with a heavy gold bracelet on my wrist. The sleigh was gliding over snowy fields, and I was peering at the skyline of the country of Canada looming in the distance. Mama and Grandmama were sitting beside me, and Papa and Dezso were in the front seat. The horses galloped and galloped, but Canada remained far, far away. Papa whipped the horses, but Canada kept receding into the distance, farther and farther, no matter how fast we traveled.

"When are we going to get there?" I asked Mama. "When

are we going to get to Canada?"

She didn't reply. She was motionless, except for a single tear trickling down the side of her face.

"When are we going to get there? When are we going to get there?" I plucked Grandmama's sleeve.

She put her finger to her lips and would not speak to me.

I poked Papa on the shoulder. He wouldn't turn around. I pulled on his jacket and yelled in his ear:

"When are we going to get to Canada?"

His head swiveled, and I fell back in horror at the sight of a grinning skull staring back at me.

"It's all right. It's all right." Somebody was stroking my arm. "It's all right. Wake up!"

I was lying in a white room full of beds. Women in white caps and uniforms, with bright Red Cross armbands, moved quietly among the patients.

"Thank God, you're back!" Sandor looked frightened.

"Where am I?"

"In a hospital, in a camp in Linz," said Sandor. "The Americans brought you here when you collapsed. You have typhus. That's why you had a headache. You were very sick, but you're over the worst of it now."

"What happened? What did the American policemen do?"

Sandor chuckled. "They just warned me never to pull anything like that again. They drove us to the hospital."

A nurse with a kind face interrupted us. She had a thermometer in her hand.

"Well, you are finally awake," she said in German. "It must be a relief to this young man. He's been pestering us for the last three days."

"I just wanted to make sure that you were all right," mumbled Sandor.

The nurse turned to him. "You'll have to leave now."

As soon as he was gone, she put the thermometer under my tongue. When she checked it a few minutes later, she seemed pleased.

"Excellent! You have no fever," she said and poured some medicine on a spoon. She laughed at the face I made when I tasted how bitter it was.

"It tastes awful, but it'll make you feel better."

Next came a sponge bath that refreshed me.

"I am sorry, but I can't change your clothing. We're short of supplies." That's when I noticed I was still wearing Frau Schmidt's dress.

"The doctor will see you later," she said, "but I'm sure he'll be satisfied with your progress. You'll be out of here in a few weeks."

She left when Sandor appeared at the foot of my bed, a bowl of gruel in his hands.

"I brought you something to eat," he said.

"I'm not hungry."

"You've got to eat, or you won't get strong." He raised the spoon.

I pushed away his hand. "I'll throw up."

"You won't!" He put the spoon back in the bowl and

stared at me angrily. "I guess you don't want to see your papa and brother again!"

I was the first to lower my eyes and reach for the bowl. "I'll have some of your stupid breakfast, and stop gloating!"

He couldn't stop himself from grinning. "Welcome back, Jutka!"

Every morning I felt stronger and more eager to find my father and my brother. It took several weeks before I was healthy enough to travel. Sandor insisted on coming with me.

I was sitting on a chair beside my bed when he appeared. He was clutching a boy's breeches, a tattered shirt, and a jacket under his arm. There was even a cap for my head, which now looked like a brush.

"This is all I could find."

"I don't mind. How did you get hold of them?"

He looked pleased with himself.

"Remember the cigarette butt I picked up out of the dirt?"

"Of course I do."

"Well, it paid for your new clothes." He passed the bundle to me. "Try them on!" he said.

I pulled the britches over my dress. They fit perfectly. The shirt and the jacket were also my size. Sandor looked me over, head to toe.

"You still look like a girl to me!" he crowed. "We should leave early tomorrow morning or we won't get on the train. They are terribly crowded."

25

Wednesday, August 1, 1945

The train station was crackling with jostling people. The air was full of excited shouting in Russian, German, Hungarian, Polish, and other languages I did not recognize. I held on tightly to Sandor's arm, my free hand clutching my belongings. There wasn't much. All I owned in the world was Frau Schmidt's dress with the pretty flowers on it, a loaf of bread, and a block of cheese.

I felt panicky at the masses of people pressing against us, but then I remembered that I was finally free, free to go anywhere I wanted, free to find my father and my brother. My heart thumped in anticipation and joy.

Our plan was to travel to Vienna by train. Sandor had earned the money for the fare by helping the Americans unload their trucks. From Vienna, we were going to make our way somehow to Andau, on the Austrian border, and cross over during the night to Csorna on the Hungarian side.

Sandor and I pushed our way through the crowd and piled into an overheated passenger car reeking of sweat. We found two empty seats on the scarred wooden benches. Next to us sat a group of farm workers with their sunburned faces, straw clinging to their clothes, the stink of fertilizer. One man was holding a loaf of bread on his lap. He tore pieces from it and handed them to his comrades. The men took swigs from an earthenware jug they passed around.

"We didn't eat this morning," said Sandor. "Are you hungry?"

Before I could reply, one of the men held out the bread.

"Help yourselves," he said in Hungarian. "It's a pleasure to meet fellow countrymen."

Sandor took the bread. He tore off a piece and passed it to me before taking one for himself.

"Thank you, sir. We're mighty hungry."

The peasant pressed the jug into Sandor's hands and he took a swig.

"That hit the spot." He wiped his mouth with the back of his hand.

"Pass the jug to your friend." The peasant winked.

"She's just recovering from typhus. Alcohol might not agree with her," said Sandor.

The men's laughter irritated me. "Of course I want a drink!"

Sandor was looking daggers at me. I took the jug out of his hands, tilted it and swallowed. Fire coursed down my throat. I coughed and spluttered.

The men laughed again.

"Good Schlivovitz will do that to you every time," the peasant said, slapping his knee. He turned to Sandor. "Where are you heading?"

"We're going home," replied Sandor. "We're from Pápa."

"We're also going home," said the man. "Good Hungarians belong in Hungary!"

The man leaned closer to us. "I heard that things are tough at home, but at least we won't have those damned Jews taking away our livelihood."

"What do you mean?" asked Sandor. His hand was like a vice on my arm.

"You know, of course, that the Jews were taken away," said the man, "and now, they're kaput!" He drew his index finger across his throat.

"I'm going to get some sleep," was all Sandor said.

We sat on the rickety train, leaning our heads against the window frame, pretending to sleep.

The train stopped several times. Groups of Russian soldiers with rifles slung over their shoulders boarded. The passengers were careful not to make eye contact with them. As we sat there motionless, I felt so exhausted that I actually fell asleep. The next thing I knew, Sandor was pulling on my arm.

"Time to get up. We're in Vienna."

We gathered up our bundles without saying good-bye to the Hungarians.

"Bastards," muttered Sandor as we stepped down onto the platform. "Are you mad at me? There were too many of them to take on."

"There was nothing you could do."

"Hold on to me," said Sandor, helping me down the last step.

Every track was full. Locomotives were belching smoke into the air. Somewhere, a whistle blew. The noise of the crowd was deafening.

"Let's go out on the street to get our bearings," said Sandor. "We'll get something to eat, and then we'll ask about going to Andau."

We headed toward the exit, careful not to collide with any Russian soldiers. As we climbed the stairs up to the street, I noticed a blond girl ahead of us. There was something familiar about the way she held herself, the way she moved. I pulled on Sandor's arm.

"We must catch that girl!" I pointed her out to him.

"Why?"

"I'll explain later! Help me!"

He elbowed his way past the people in our path much to their dismay. I followed. We were almost at the exit when we caught up with the girl. I reached over the head of the woman in front of me and tapped the girl on the shoulder. She swung around. It was Miri.

*

Sandor ordered three espressos from the waitress.

We were sitting in an outdoor café down the street from the railway station. I kept staring at Miri, afraid that if I took my eyes off her she would disappear. She must have felt the same for she was grasping my fingers so tightly that they were going numb.

"I can't believe I ran into you!" she kept repeating.

"Neither can I. I want to know everything that has happened to you since you and your mother disappeared. What are you doing in Vienna? Do you have news of my papa and my brother?"

She let go of my fingers. "Mama and I went into hiding with the partisans in the forests of Yugoslavia, but we were captured a few months later and sent to Bergen-Belsen." She picked up her cup and set it down again without drinking. "I lost my mother there. When the war ended, I went home. Nobody came back except me."

I drew my chair close to her. "I'm so sorry! Do you know anything about my father and my brother? They were with your father." I was afraid to say more and afraid to ask.

"Don't go back," she said by way of reply.

"I have to find them. I want my father!" She squeezed my fingers tighter.

"Your papa and your brother won't be coming back . . . nor will my father," she said. "All three of them were shot."

I felt hot and cold and dizzy at the same time. I pulled away from her and jumped to my feet. I could not understand why she was saying such terrible things to me.

"You're lying!"

"I wish I was. I met somebody who saw it happen."

Sandor pulled me back to my seat. "Hush, Jutka! Listen to what Miri has to say."

"I am so sorry, but it's true. Please believe me!" pleaded Miri. Tears flooded her eyes. "I wish I didn't have to tell you this. They were exhausted. They'd been digging ditches for long hours, and when they were so tired that they couldn't carry on, they sat down in the shade of a tree for a moment. A guard noticed and shot them – in the head."

I stopped listening. My mind was flooded with a thousand images – Papa swinging me high in the air when I was a little girl; Papa telling me how much he loved me. And Dezso, my big brother – how he looked out for me; how much we laughed during the hours we spent over the chessboard. I thought of Shabbos dinners – Mama's hands dancing over the candles, her lips moving in prayer. I thought of Papa blessing the wine and the Shabbos bread gracing our table. I thought of the pleasure on Mama's face when we praised her cooking. I thought of my brother's laughter when he teased me. I was so lost in grief that I barely understood Sandor's gentle voice.

"Do you still want to go back? Think it over carefully. It seems to me that there is nothing for either of us back there."

"Nor for me," added Miri.

"Agi . . . what happened to Agi?" I was desperate. "Did she make it home, Miri?"

Miri shook her head.

"Auschwitz was liberated months before Mauthausen," said Sandor. "Don't you think that if she survived, you'd know?"

I clamped my hands over my ears. "Stop it! Stop it!"

Sandor took my hands and held them tightly. "You have to face the truth."

"Agi has to get home!" I cried. "Someone has to have survived!"

He shook his head. "Face it. We have no homes. I was prepared to go back with you, but that's because you wanted to. There is nothing for us there. There is only one place that will be my home. Eretz Israel!"

Miri agreed. "That's why I left Hungary."

A Russian soldier sauntered by, close to our table. He gave a black-toothed smile to Miri. She shuddered and hugged herself before continuing to speak.

"It's terrible," she said. "The neighbors kept asking, 'Where is your mama? It's too bad your papa didn't come home.' They all said, 'We didn't know what they were doing to you!' Nobody in the whole country seems to know what was going on," she said bitterly.

"They were furious when I asked for our belongings. I saw my mother's crystal vase on Mrs. Kristof's dining-room table and she denied that it was ever ours. Mrs. Kristof was no different from the rest of them." She shook her head. "Klari was the only person who was kind to me, and it wasn't easy for her. Her parents forbade her to have anything to do with me. She had to sneak out to see me."

I stole a glance at Sandor. "What about Tamas?"

Miri shifted in her seat. "I kept as far away from him as I could. At first, he belonged to the Arrow Cross. Now that the Russians are there, he's a Communist."

"Who is Tamas?" Sandor asked.

I kept silent.

"He is our friend Klari's brother. He used to chum around with Jutka's brother."

I shot her a grateful look.

"I should never have tried to go back. When I decided to leave for good, I got help through the Bricha."

"The Bricha?" I asked.

"Zionists who are helping Jews leave Europe and go to Eretz Israel. They arranged everything. Sandor is right, Jutka. I'm going to Eretz Israel too."

As they talked, I thought of a horsedrawn sleigh skimming over the crisp, pure snow. That's when I knew.

"Agi and I always wanted to go to Canada. I have family in Canada – my papa's cousin."

"Canada," Miri said, "so far away. Are you sure?"

The waitress appeared and set three small cups of steaming espresso in front of us. We drank deeply.

"How I have missed good coffee!" Sandor turned to me. "What do you want to do, Jutka? When we're in Linz, you can decide where you want to live."

"I'm not going to Linz. I want to go to Landsberg in the American region," Miri said. "They've set up a DP camp, and we can get free food and lodging there while we wait."

"Wait for what?" I said. We had waited forever, it seemed.

"To go to Eretz Israel."

"Or to Canada . . ." I said.

"Or to Canada," she agreed. "Come to Landsberg with me."

I was lost. I had been torn from the home I loved. Everybody who had cared about me was dead. There was no one waiting for me to return home. I realized that home had vanished. It was a dream more distant than Canada.

"All right, Miri, we'll go with you to Landsberg," I said.

26

Wednesday, August 1, 1945 – Thursday, August 2, 1945

The sun was low on the horizon when we arrived at the Landsberg Displaced Persons Camp. My heart sank when I saw the barbed wire on top of the iron fence that enclosed it. It looked like a concentration camp.

"Sandor, are we crazy to do this willingly?"

Sandor was talking to an American soldier with a rifle slung over his shoulder. One of the sentries escorted us to a building for registration. A woman wearing a badge that said UNRRA was waiting for us behind a table piled high with documents.

"Welcome to Landsberg," she said. "My name is Margaret. I work for the United Nations Relief and Rehabilitation Administration. Don't hesitate to ask me any questions."

We remained silent.

She helped us fill out documents. When we finished, she picked up a spray can from the table and stood up. Sandor went first. Next it was my turn. I closed my eyes and held my hands in front of my mouth while she sprayed me with DDT. Miri came after me. I was glad that I was wearing trousers when she sprayed the DDT under Miri's skirt.

The woman apologized. "I am sorry, but we must do this to kill any lice."

She passed us on to her colleague.

"It's a good thing that you have reasonably good clothes," the second UNRRA lady said. "Our supplies are low."

She gave each of us cooking and eating utensils, soap, and a prickly army blanket.

"Now go to that man," she pointed. "He is with the American Joint Distribution Committee. That's a mouthful. We call it the Joint."

The man led us to the camp kitchen. I don't know what I expected, but it wasn't the dirt on the floor and the filth covering the counters and the pots and pans. A cook with a messy apron and even dirtier hands dipped a ladle into a huge metal cauldron simmering on the stove. He filled our bowls with a green liquid.

"Pea soup," he explained. "It's the best we can do right now." He laughed and handed each of us a slice of cornbread. "To sop up the soup."

The Joint official looked at the documents we had been issued, and he led us toward red brick barracks in the distance.

Sandor was told to go to the men's building, while Miri and I were assigned to the women's block.

We climbed up to the second floor and were taken into a large room divided into cubicles by tall, wooden lockers.

"We try to group our residents according to nationality," our guide explained. "Many of the women here are Hungarian, and most of them are Jewish but not all."

He stopped in front of a cubicle. "Your new home," he said with a kind smile.

The room contained a bunk bed made of rough wood, a battered table, and two upturned boxes that served as chairs. There was a hot plate on the table. We stowed our belongings in the lockers, and the official left.

Miri sat on the bottom bunk. She bounced up and down on the bed.

"A palace!" She laughed. "Can I be on the top bunk?"

"Sure."

"Hello, girls," a reedy voice said in Hungarian.

A woman with a wizened face stood beside our table. Her shabby dress hung on her skeletal frame. Her face was so worn that it was impossible to guess her age. She was coughing so hard that she had difficulty completing a sentence.

"Where are you from?" she wheezed.

"Pápa," Miri answered.

"I am from Komarom. My name is Andrea Forster." She stopped to make a hollow whooping sound. "My daughter and I were in Auschwitz. Her name is Magda. Did either of you meet anybody by that name?"

I shook my head. She stared at me.

"You look like my Magda." She turned on her heels, as if saying another word would have taken too much out of her.

The woman in the next cubicle stuck her head out from behind the locker.

"Is Andrea still looking for her daughter?"

I nodded.

"She'll never find her. Her daughter was sent to the left. But did you run into my Jolan? Jolan Vidor from Gyor? She was in Auschwitz."

Her face fell when I told her no. Others began to shout out names and where they were from. Everyone wanted to know if we had any news about their missing relatives.

"Lili Krausz from Balatonfured? She was in Auschwitz."

"What about Moishe Stern from Paszto? Do you know where he is?"

Over and over we explained that we had no news. I thought my heart would break because I knew that we were killing hope. Except for Andrea's hacking cough, the room was silent once again.

I wanted to wash up before changing into Frau Schmidt's dress. The bathroom was at the end of the hall. The corridor leading to it was lit by a dingy lightbulb, but even in the gloom I saw that the floor was littered with rotting food. My stomach turned when I saw human excrement along the walls.

The bathrooms were so foul that my stomach gave a mighty heave, and I wretched into a toilet. The sinks were plugged with stinking scraps – people had tried to wash their dishes in them. I had to try several taps before I found one that worked to wash my hands and face. I wiped my hands on my trousers and my face on my sleeve.

Miri was waiting for me in the cubicle. "What's the matter? Why are you so pale?" she asked.

"I threw up. The bathrooms are revolting! Don't go!"

She laughed.

"I have no choice."

I changed into my dress. I smoothed down my hair and used the edge of the documents that Margaret, the UNRRA lady, had given me to clean my nails.

When Miri came back, we went to look for Sandor. We didn't have to go far. He was in front of our building with a group of young people. Some of them were leaning against the building, others sat on the ground. Most of them were wearing their concentration camp pajamas. They were listening intently to a man in a British soldier's uniform with a Star of David on his sleeve.

Sandor moved over to make room for us, and we sat beside him on the ground.

"I was waiting for you," he said. "Meet my new friend." A stocky young man was seated beside him. He smiled and shook our hands.

"My name is Natan Weiszmann."

"I am Jutka."

"And I am Miri."

She smiled at him widely. Natan's ears turned crimson.

Sandor pulled me close to him.

The soldier was speaking in Hebrew, pausing so that a boy could translate his words into Hungarian.

"Eretz Israel awaits you," said the soldier. "Eretz Israel is the homeland for Jews like you and me. As you know, the British are preventing your return to your homeland. That's why we're here."

"What do you mean?" asked Miri.

"The Jewish Brigade is here to help you get to our homeland. I came to Landsberg to make your dreams come true."

"How?" asked Natan.

"It's best not to reveal our plans openly," said the soldier, "but be assured that we know what we're doing."

"They are going to take us by ship to Eretz Israel and then smuggle us into the country without the British knowing," whispered Sandor.

The soldier had finished speaking. A young man stood up and squeezed out "Hava Nagila" on a battered accordion. We clasped hands and formed a circle. We danced slowly at first and then faster and faster. When we finally stopped, I had to bend over to catch my breath. I felt strange. It took me a while to realize that what I was feeling was happiness for the first time in ages.

After breakfast the next morning, we registered with UNRRA and the International Red Cross to trace our families. Hope is an odd creature. I knew that it was foolish, but I kept on hoping that Miri's information was wrong, and by some miracle Papa and Dezso were still alive and were waiting for me in another DP camp. I explained to the officials that my name would not be on lists of survivors released from Auschwitz-Birkenau because I had lied when we were tattooed and registered in the concentration camp. I had said that my name was Judit Freis in order to be allowed to stay with my friends. This meant that if any of my relatives survived the war, they wouldn't know that I was alive. I would have to find them myself on the lists of survivors published daily in the camp newspapers or on the radio program that listed the names of survivors seeking their relatives.

Once we'd finished registering, the warm July day yawned ahead. Miri stayed behind with Natan while Sandor and I walked aimlessly. The size of the camp amazed me. Its littered, makeshift streets rang with different languages. It was easy to see that the camp housed both Jews and non-Jews and that the two groups were quite separate from each other.

The sun warmed our faces and cast a golden glow over the shabby buildings. Sandor and I held hands. When we arrived at the fence surrounding the camp, we had to stop. We gazed outside through the barbed wire and the golden glow evaporated. Across the street, well-dressed people were strolling and enjoying the summer weather.

"You'd think they won the war," said Sandor. "They're outside and we're still in here."

I watched a young couple stoop to admire a puppy on a leather leash. The plump girl's long curtain of hair hung to her shoulders. Her beau leaned his head forward and whispered something in her ear. I couldn't hear what he was saying, but her trilling laugh echoed over to us. She seemed so much younger than I felt, than I would ever feel again.

Sandor ruffled my hair. "Curly top," he said.

"My hair is too short."

"It'll grow," he said. "You're still pretty."

I punched him in the arm. "Liar!"

"It's true," he said, pulling me so close to him that I could hear his stomach grumble. "Sorry!" He grinned. "I'm hungry." He looked up. "The sun's almost overhead. It must be noon. Let's get some lunch."

We set out for the camp kitchen. As we turned the corner, our way was blocked by women shrieking and throwing stones at a lone figure in the middle of the crowd. The blond head of the woman in the middle was lowered, so I couldn't see her face.

"Murderer! You killed my Esther!" cried a woman as she flung a rock at the cowering figure.

"You deserve to die, you beast!"

"Die, Kapo! Die, Kapo!"

The woman in the center raised her head. Our eyes met. It was the Kapo of my block from Auschwitz. She was dressed in rags, and her face was gaunt, but it was her.

My memories overwhelmed me: the contempt in her voice when she cursed me, the hours we spent at Appell, the bite of her baton when she took me to the Lagerführer's office to be put to death. I remembered her leer when she condemned Eva to die. I remembered and remembered. I knew that I could never, would never, forget. As if in a trance, I bent, picked up a stone, and threw it. It hit her arm.

"No, Jutka, no!" cried Sandor.

I ignored him. I picked up another stone and raised my arm. He caught my wrist. The crowd parted and three GIs appeared. One of them shot his rifle into the air and ordered us to leave. We scattered. I held on to Sandor's arm, the stone tightly clutched in my fist. When we arrived at the building that housed the kitchen, I let it drop to the ground.

"I am glad the soldiers came," I told Sandor. "I don't know if I could have stopped myself."

27

Saturday, october 20, 1945 — Tuesday, october 30, 1945

The DP camp was run by UNRRA and the U.S. army. When Major Irving Heymont, the head of the new American battalion, arrived in early October, the camp went through an incredible transformation. Heymont ordered the removal of the barbed wire from the top of the fence surrounding the camp. From then on, our own camp police guarded the gate. Best of all, we did not have to get passes from the Americans to leave the camp. It felt wonderful and scary at the same time to know that we could come and go as we pleased. The non-Jewish residents were transferred to other DP camps or were sent home. Most of them had families waiting for them. I was glad to see them go. Many of them had collaborated with the Nazis. It was difficult to live with people who hated us with such a passion.

The men formed work brigades that spent hours with shovels and wheelbarrows cleaning the streets of the camp. Miri and I scrubbed and swept and washed with our block-mates until our building shone.

I never found a single familiar name on the camp newspaper lists of survivors. Surely I couldn't be the only one in my family to have survived! There had to be somebody else besides me. Nobody, nobody. Margaret from the UNRRA office had given me writing paper, a pencil, a few envelopes, and stamps. I sat down on one of the wooden boxes by the rickety table in our cubicle and tried to think who I could contact in Hungary. At first, I was going to write to Klari to tell her that I was alive, but I was afraid that my letter would be intercepted by her parents or by Tamas. The only other person I could think of was Julia, Agi's housekeeper. Julia had been kind to us.

> October 20, 1945
> Landsberg DP Center
> Landsberg, Germany

Dear Julia,
You may be surprised to hear from someone you must have thought was dead, but I am happy to tell you that I am very much alive. I am writing to you, Julia, because I have no one else to turn to.
My beloved mama and grandmama perished in Auschwitz. Mrs. Grazer was with them. My only

consolation is that they did not know the fate that awaited them. My old friend Miri Schwarz is with me in Landsberg. She heard that my papa and my brother were killed in their forced labor regiment. I am hoping that you will tell me that her information is wrong, that both Papa and Dezso have returned home.

I am also searching for my beloved Agi. She and I were together in Auschwitz until she saved my life at a terrible cost to herself. I don't know if she survived her injuries. Please let me know if you have any news of her.

Please, please, Julia, answer my letter as soon as possible. I feel so alone. I keep asking why I survived while my loved ones lost their lives.

I miss my home, Julia. I wish everything could be as it was before the war, but I know that can never be.

I will never forget how kind you were to us in our hour of need.

Yours affectionately,
Jutka Weltner

My second letter was to Papa's cousin who had sent my family the package from Canada:

October 20, 1945
Landsberg DP Camp
Landsberg, Germany

My dear cousin,

You must be surprised to hear from a person you have never met. I am your cousin Judit, the fifteen-year-old daughter of your cousin Armin Weltner. Please call me Jutka. Everybody does.

I am writing to you from Germany. I spent the last sixteen months in Auschwitz and Mauthausen and am presently in a DP camp in Landsberg. I am desperate to leave the camp, but I have no place to go.

I am all alone in the world, cousin. My entire family is lost. You are the only blood kin I have left. I cannot tell you how precious this connection is to me.

Ever since you were kind enough to send us a parcel before we were deported from Hungary, I cannot get the idea of Canada out of my mind. I read and reread the book you sent us about your wonderful country. When I no longer had the book to read, I dreamt about it.

Cousin, I want to go to Canada. If I went to Canada, I wouldn't be alone. I would be close to you, my only living relative. I am begging you to please help me realize my dream. I am

hardworking and conscientious. I will do anything not to make you regret your generosity.

I hope to hear from you soon.

Yours sincerely,
Your cousin, Jutka Weltner

I put both letters into envelopes and sealed them. I had
Julia's address, but the mail was not reliable in Hungary. I
knew that Iren lived in Ottawa, but I had no street address.
I wondered if either letter would ever be read. If they were and
anyone answered out of the void, it would help me decide
where I wanted to go. I would make up my mind only after I
received their replies. I didn't tell Sandor about the letters.

I looked at the clock ticking on the wall. If I hurried, I
would still have time to give my letters to Margaret before
the day's mail left the camp.

"One more time, and this time faster!" barked Ari, the shaliach from Palestine. He was a member of the Hagana, and he
had replaced the soldier from the Jewish Brigade who had
spoken to us when we arrived. Ari had us marching every
morning. I didn't mind.

"Good work, Weltner," Ari said as I puffed through the
finish line near the back of the group.

"But I am slow!"

"That doesn't matter. You try hard. I want to see you on
track-and-field day."

That seemed unlikely. My days were full. In addition to cleaning up the camp and marching and exercising every morning to prepare us for Eretz Israel, we studied Hebrew and Jewish history with Ari. But it was for a future that made no sense to me. It was as if someone had erased me – my name, my home, my country.

Ari was confident. "When the time comes, you will know what's right for you. You'll realize that Eretz Israel is the only place for a Jewish girl."

His certainty confused me. I marched and studied and hoped I would make the right decision. I knew that I didn't want to be parted from Sandor and Miri. I wanted to see Eretz Israel flourish, but I dreamt of Canada, all cold and pure and covered in snow. I had had that dream when Mama was alive, and if I gave it up, my old life would vanish.

Although I liked Hebrew classes, the most exciting part of my days was in the afternoon when I attended regular school. It was wonderful to be learning again. Math was still a struggle, but a dignified old man, Professor Berger, taught us literature. We had few books, so we relied on his memory. It was when I listened to his musical voice reciting poetry that I felt my soul begin to heal.

School had been canceled because the first democratic elections were being held in the camp. I was too young to vote, but my blockmates had all gone to elect the new camp committee. I lay on my bed, relishing the quiet.

I must have been dozing, because I was startled to see Andrea. She was at the foot of the bunk with a suitcase in her hand, dressed in a threadbare coat. She wheezed and covered her mouth. Andrea had taken a liking to me. I was the only person she spoke to and that wasn't often. Usually she would just come into the cubicle, sit down silently, and stare at me. At first, it rattled me, but after a while, I got so used to her that I forgot she was there.

"I came to say good-bye."

I sat up. "Where are you going?"

She perched on the edge of my mattress.

"I'm going to find Magda," she said. "She is all I've got. She must be in another DP camp in the American zone."

"But, Andrea," I said softly, "you know that you won't be able to find her. You know that she was sent to the left in Auschwitz."

Her voice became strident. "I don't believe it! Magda must be alive! She would never leave me! She may be sick and waiting for me to find her."

"No!" I shook my head for emphasis. I wasn't doing her a favor by feeding her fantasies. "I like to think that my papa and brother are alive too, but I know better. We must face reality!"

She stood up straight. "You don't understand . . ."

Footsteps pounded on the wooden floor and Sandor appeared. His vitality filled the cubicle, making it feel smaller than ever.

He grabbed my hands, pulled me up, and danced me around the tiny space.

"You'll never guess who is coming to our camp!"

"Who?"

"David Ben Gurion!" He spun me around. "Isn't it unbelievable?"

"Why would the head of the Jewish Agency in Palestine be coming to Landsberg?"

"I don't know, but he is on his way here from Munich."

I turned to Andrea, but she was gone.

A cheering crowd lined both sides of the road. There were so many people that I couldn't see David Ben Gurion until he climbed onto a podium. Women held out bouquets of flowers to him while men waited to shake his hand. He was a small man, but I forgot his size as soon as he began to speak. He told us that Eretz Israel was our ancestral home and that Eretz Israel needed us. He asked us to be patient and not to lose hope. We would reach the promised land. Our voices rose in "Hatikva." We sang:

> In the Jewish heart
> A Jewish spirit still sings,
>
> And the eyes look east
> Toward Zion

Our hope is not lost,
Our hope of two thousand years,

To be a free nation in our land,
In the land of Zion and Jerusalem.

The music washed over me and entered my soul. I felt at peace. I looked at Sandor. Tears were running down his cheeks.

When it was time to return to our blocks, Sandor was exultant.

"What a day!" he cried. "David Ben Gurion!"

"He's right. We belong in Eretz Israel." As soon as I said the words, I felt as if a heavy load had been lifted off my shoulders.

Sandor grabbed my arms and looked deep into my eyes. "Do you mean it, Jutka? Don't say it if you don't mean it!"

"I mean it. I'll go with you. I promise."

We said good-bye. I climbed up to the second floor and went to look for Andrea, but she had already left the camp.

28

Sunday, January 20, 1946 – Sunday, February 24, 1946

Winter came. We were living in a twilight – waiting and hoping. The war was over, but not for us. When I looked in the mirror, I didn't recognize the person staring back at me. I wasn't a girl, and I wasn't a woman. I was no one's daughter or sister. I almost forgot what it was like to live in an ordinary house on a street like a thousand others.

Slowly, I grew to accept that I was alone in the world. No one was looking for me. I hadn't received a reply from Julia in Hungary or Iren in Canada. I found that I could keep the past at bay by working. I went to classes, and I got a job playing the piano four nights a week in the camp's café. I wasn't paid, but the man who ran the café gave me cigarettes once in a while. Cigarettes served as the camp's currency. It was enough just to be able to play the piano.

One dark winter night, I found Miri waiting for me at the back door of the café. The manager did not allow our friends to wait for us inside. Miri was stamping her feet and rubbing her hands together in a vain attempt to keep warm.

"I thought that you'd never finish work!" she said.

I hugged her. I did not see her often. She spent most of her time with Natan. I drew her arm through mine, and we set out for the block.

"I have to talk to you." Her eyes were shining.

She sat down on the bed and patted the mattress beside her.

"Something wonderful has happened to me," she said. "Can you guess what I am going to tell you?"

I shook my head.

She beamed. "I am going to have a baby!"

I heard her words, but they did not register. "What did you say?"

"I am going to have a baby," she said again. She did a happy little jig. "I'm going to have a baby! I'm going to have a baby!"

When I finally found my voice, I realized that I had to choose my words carefully.

"You can't have a baby," I said. "You're only a year older than me, and you're not married."

"So what? They didn't get us, Jutka. This is a life! We've won! Besides, I love Natan. We are going to get married." She grabbed my hands. "Be happy for me! I want this baby more than anything else in the world. Can you believe it?

I'll have a baby and a husband. I'll have a family again. I won't be alone anymore!"

"You're not alone, Miri. You have me." I knew this wasn't what she meant even as I said it.

"I know that. You're my best friend in the world. Friends are important, but they're different from having your own family. Please, Jutka, be happy for me," she begged. "Will you help me plan my wedding?"

I didn't know how to reply. I felt happy and sad at the same time. All kinds of ideas crowded into my head, but I did not express them. I did not say that her parents would be disappointed in her. I did not say that I regretted the loss of her freedom. I did not say that I felt sorry for the weight of the adult responsibilities she was so eagerly embracing. To be honest, I was also jealous. At the same time, I was happy that she would love and be loved in return. I kissed her cheek and said, "Of course I'll help. How long do we have to plan your wedding?"

Two weeks later on a bright February afternoon, we set up a makeshift wedding canopy in the square in front of the block. A crowd had gathered for the ceremony even though most days at least one wedding took place in the camp. Despite the cool weather, Miri had refused to wear a coat. She looked beautiful in the frilly white blouse and white skirt I had bought in exchange for the cigarettes I got for playing the piano. It was my wedding present to her. Her face was covered by a short white veil Margaret had made out of the curtains that had covered the windows in her office in the UNRRA building.

I felt self-conscious in the plain shirt and dark skirt I was wearing, but I knew that nobody was looking at me. All eyes were on the bride.

We walked slowly, arm in arm, toward the huppah. From the corner of my eye, I could see Sandor leading Natan, resplendent in a borrowed suit and tall black hat, toward the marriage canopy.

A fiddler began to play a Hassidic tune that tugged at my heart strings. I peeked at Miri. She was smiling broadly under her veil.

"Are you sure you want to do this?" I whispered to her.

"I've never been more certain of anything in my entire life," she replied. "I only wish that my mama and papa were here to see me."

"They are." I squeezed her arm.

We reached the wedding canopy. Miri stepped forward and took her place beside Natan. I stood beside Sandor. He took my hand.

"This will be us some day," he whispered.

The rabbi began his blessings, so I didn't have to answer him.

Sandor treated the four of us to a wedding supper in a little restaurant in town called the Drei Husaren.

The dining room looked romantic. A candle flickering in the middle of the lace-covered table cast dancing shadows over our faces. The restaurant was crowded, but there was an empty table next to ours. Two violinists were walking among the customers, pausing for tips.

We studied the menus.

"Everything is terribly expensive," said Natan.

"Nothing is too expensive for my best friend's wedding supper," replied Sandor.

Miri looked around the restaurant. "This is a beautiful place. Thank you so much for bringing us here," she said to Sandor.

Sandor smiled. Only I knew the long hours he had worked on a construction crew in town to pay for the evening.

"All the other ladies are so fashionable that they make me feel shabby," said Miri.

I adjusted her veil. She had kept it on because she said that it made her feel like a bride. I straightened the collar of my own blouse, but I knew that nothing could make it look more glamorous.

The waiter ushered a couple to the table next to ours. The tall blond girl must have been our age; the distinguished-looking man with her was much older. The girl's eyes raked over us.

"I don't want to sit next to DPs! They stink!" she said loudly. Her eyes rested on Miri's veil. "Is that cow supposed to be a bride?"

I saw Miri's downcast eyes and the flush over Natan's face as he jumped up from his chair. I stood up too and put a restraining hand on his arm.

"How dare you speak like that about my friend!" I said before Natan could open his mouth.

Natan sat back down.

The girl ignored me.

"Surely you don't expect us to sit next to Jews?" she said to the waiter.

Her companion chuckled.

"Of course not, Fräulein Schiller, of course not." The waiter flicked a linen napkin.

"If you cater to such riffraff, I will tell my friends not to dine here."

"I am so sorry, Fräulein Schiller, but we did not know who they were when they made their reservation," explained the waiter.

He bowed so low that I was waiting for his nose to hit his knees. He turned to us.

"You must leave immediately!"

"What do you mean?" asked Sandor. "I booked this table days ago."

"Please leave!"

"Get out of here!" barked the old man. "Just because the Führer didn't get all of you, don't think that you are welcome here!"

Sandor and Natan jumped up, hands balled into fists.

"Stop it!" I said. "I won't let you ruin Miri's wedding day."

I turned to the waiter. "Sir, this is my friends' wedding supper. We don't want any trouble. Please, sir, let us stay here."

Tears were running down Miri's face.

"No, Jutka," she said. "I don't want to stay where we're not wanted. Let's go, my husband."

Miri and I dragged the boys to the exit. At the door, I looked back. The last thing I saw was the smug expression on the blond girl's face as she sat down at the table next to ours.

29

Sunday, March 10, 1946 – Sunday, March 24, 1946

The snow had melted and the air had softened. Buds had appeared on the trees. The sight of new life around me was sweet. I wouldn't allow myself to dwell on old dreams.

In mid-March, we all came down with a mysterious malady – Purim fever. It all began when the camp newspaper, the *Landsberger Lager-Cajtung*, proclaimed Sunday, March 17, to Sunday, March 24, a workers' and Purim carnival. Prizes were to be given to the best decorated building and the most beautiful window. Everybody began to build floats, sew costumes, and plan parades.

"What should we wear?" asked Miri. She cupped her rounded belly and patted it. "I am too fat to be Queen Esther."

"You'll make a gorgeous queen," I said.

She laughed.

"Thank you for saying it. We'll have to find some material to make costumes, and that's going to be hard."

"Let's ask the nurses at the hospital if they would sell us two sheets. They're soft and white and would make lovely costumes," I said. "I can pay in cigarettes."

Miri heaved herself to her feet. "Let's go before somebody else has the same idea."

We wanted to celebrate being alive. Music blared from radio loudspeakers. All of the buildings were decorated with banners, slogans, and caricatures. Someone hoisted up effigies of Hitler. We hanged him and hanged him, over and over again.

We made our way through the crowd of Queen Esthers and Hamans and Ahasueruses. Some people were wearing their concentration camp uniforms. A man had dressed as Hitler.

The nurses wouldn't take my cigarettes, but they gave us two sheets. Miri and I had draped ourselves in them. We felt like glamorous Queen Esthers, with silver paper crowns on our heads. Sandor and Natan made handsome Ahasueruses, with army blankets thrown over their shoulders as capes.

The four of us held hands to prevent the crowd from separating us as we found our way to the field to look at floats. We listened to speeches and a reading of the Megillah.

I felt playful and carefree and very young when Miri suddenly began to cry.

"What's the matter, sweetheart?" asked Natan.

"Last year, on Purim, my mama and papa were still alive." Miri sobbed into her hands.

"So were my father and brother." I burrowed my head in Sandor's chest. "We're alive and they're gone. Do you ever wonder why we survived and they didn't?"

Sandor stroked my hair. "We'll never know why, but we're here and Hitler, may his name be forever blotted out, is hanging on the scaffold!" He looked at the battered effigy.

A man elbowed his way through the throng toward us. It was Ari, the shaliach.

"I am glad I found you," he said, out of breath. "I need your help."

"What's going on?" asked Sandor.

Ari whispered something into Sandor's ear. I heard the words *shipment* and *Hagana*.

Sandor nodded. "We'll be there. What time do you need us?"

"After nightfall." Ari melted into the crowd.

"What did he say?" I asked.

"What's going on, Natan?" echoed Miri.

Sandor and Natan exchanged glances.

"We can't tell you," replied Sandor. "Not yet."

"All we can say is that it's for Eretz Israel," mumbled Natan.

"I want to help!" said Miri. "Tell me what's going on!"

Sandor waited while the crowd roared at the sight of a beautifully decorated float.

"Ari doesn't want us to discuss it with you," said Sandor when the float had passed, "but you are welcome to come along."

We pushed our way past revelers to a warehouse at the edge of a field, beside the fence surrounding the camp. The building had no windows and most of the front wall consisted of two large metal doors.

Sandor rapped sharply on one of them. An eye appeared at a peephole, and we heard loud clanging, banging, and the sound of a key scraping in a lock. We followed Ari into the warehouse. Sandor helped him slide the metal doors shut.

Dozens of Queen Esthers, Mordechais, Ahasueruses, and a few Hamans sat at long wooden tables. I recognized most of them. They were either taking rifles apart, cleaning rifle parts, or reassembling the weapons. We found empty chairs at the table closest to us.

"What's going on here?" I asked.

"These guns will be shipped to Eretz Israel," said the girl next to me, "to the Hagana."

She stopped talking when Ari came over.

"Thank you for coming to help," he said. "We were lucky to lay our hands on this shipment. We need all the manpower we can get."

He sat down next to Sandor and showed us how to take apart the rifles, clean and polish their parts, and then reassemble them.

"The weapons are old," he said. "It's very important that they be in perfect working order. It might mean the difference between life and death for one of us."

Sandor and I worked together. I lost count of how many rifles we reassembled. My shoulders and neck began to ache from hunching over the guns. When we finished, we packed the weapons into wooden crates. Ari checked his watch. As if on cue, there was a knock on the door. The soldier from the Jewish Brigade who had addressed us months earlier was waiting in the dark outside. Two more members of the Jewish Brigade stood beside him. Three tarpaulin-covered army trucks were parked outside of the fence, their lights off. More Jewish Brigade soldiers were waiting by the trucks.

We passed the crates over the fence to the soldiers, who loaded the weapons into the trucks. We worked quickly and silently in the moonlight. When all the guns were aboard the vehicles, the trucks drove away into the night.

30

Thursday, April 25, 1946

A rowdy group at the café kept me playing the piano later than usual. It was past eleven o'clock when I stepped into the still street lit by a pale moon. The spring air was earthy and full of promise. When I got to the block, I was careful not to make noise as I climbed the steps to my floor.

The vast dormitory was dark except for one cubicle at the end of the room. I heard the sound of weeping. The women were gathered around a slight figure in a bed. A girl tugged on my sleeve.

"Ah, you're finally back! She returned an hour ago."

"You're the only one she wants to see," a woman explained. She shook her head. "It doesn't look good . . ."

"What do you mean?"

I made my way to the bed. It was Andrea. I took her hand.

"I am so glad that you came back," I said.

"You have the same smile," she responded.

She paused, her body racked by loud, wrenching coughs. She grasped my fingers tightly.

"I couldn't find her," she finally said. "I looked everywhere, but my Magda is gone."

She closed her eyes, and her fingers grew slack in my grip. She, too, was gone.

3 1

Sunday, May 12, 1946

" **J** utka! Jutka! Wait up!"

I was on the way to the sports field to cheer for Sandor's soccer team when Margaret caught up with me. She was waving a letter.

"I am so glad that I saw you," she panted. "I went to your barracks, but you had already left." She handed me the letter. "I thought it might be important."

The stamp on the envelope was from Canada. I turned over the letter, my heart racing. Iren Weltner's name and address were on the back.

"It's from my papa's cousin in Canada."

"Are you feeling all right? You're white as a ghost."

"I am fine . . . It's just that it's . . . I wrote to her months ago. I didn't have her full address. When she didn't reply, I thought that she didn't receive my letter."

"I'll leave you to read it," she said, patting me on the shoulder. "I hope it's good news."

I sat down on a bench under a tree, by the fence. I held the envelope in my hand for a long time. What if my cousin wrote that she would help me get to Canada? For a moment, I slipped into that dreamland of open spaces and snowy mountains. I shook my head to clear it. I had promised Sandor that I would go to Eretz Israel with him. I loved Sandor. I would not disappoint him. I wanted to rip up the letter and throw away the pieces. But my fingers seemed to have a mind of their own, and before I realized what I was doing, I tore the envelope open and began to read:

> 835 Queenston Bay
> Ottawa, Canada
> April 13, 1946

My dear cousin Jutka,

I was so happy to hear from you. It took a long while for your letter to reach me. Please note my correct mailing address.

I want to express my sorrow and deepest sympathy to you for the loss of your beloved family, including your dear father. Although I never met your papa in person (my father was a very young man when he immigrated to Canada, and I was born here), I heard wonderful things about him.

Even though a vast ocean separated our fathers, my father never lost his love for his young cousin.

As soon as I mail this letter off to you, I will take the necessary steps to arrange for your immigration. I am more than happy to sponsor you or act as a guarantor for you – whatever the immigration people require of me I will do.

I await you with open arms. I, too, am alone in the world. I, too, have lost my parents. You and I are the sole remaining members of our family. We should be together. I look forward to hearing from you.

Yours affectionately,
Your cousin, Iren Weltner

I stared at the letter for several moments. The hand that had written it shared my blood. I crumpled it up in my fist, ready to throw it away, but then I changed my mind and stuffed it into my pocket. I must keep it so I'll have Iren's address. I'll write her when I get to Eretz Israel, I reassured myself.

After the first half-hour, it was obvious that not only would we lose but that we would lose badly to the team that had arrived in army trucks from the Feldafing DP Camp. I climbed down from the bleachers and walked toward the track that ran the circumference of the sports field. Ari was talking animatedly to a group of girls in shorts, shirts, and track shoes.

"Have you decided to join the track team, Jutka?" he asked.

"I was just watching the soccer match."

The girls looked me over, assessing me as if I were a new racehorse.

"Come on, run with us, Jutka," said Ari. "You'll have a good time." He laughed. "It beats seeing our boys flattened by the team from Feldafing."

The Feldafing side of the bleachers was going wild, clapping their hands and stomping their feet at another goal.

"See what I mean?" asked Ari.

The last time I had run was during the grotesque race in Auschwitz.

"Come on," said Ari.

Reluctantly, I lined up at the starting line and kicked off my leather shoes. I felt out of place in my summer dress and bare feet.

"If you want to join the team, I'll get you track shoes," offered Ari. "They're secondhand, but they'll do."

"It won't be easy. I have big feet." The two girls beside me laughed.

"My name is Anna," said the taller girl.

"I am Marika," said her friend, shaking my hand.

"Be careful not to start running before Ari says 'Go!'" said Anna.

Butterflies began to dance in the pit of my stomach.

"How many times are we supposed to go around the track?"

Marika smiled. "You really are a novice! We're training for the 1,500 meters, so we must run around three and three-quarter times."

"Quiet!" cried Ari. "Get ready! Go!"

I ran at an easy pace at first, not even feeling out of breath. At the end of the first lap, three of the eight girls, including Marika, fell behind. Anna was at the front of the four runners ahead of me. I upped the pace a bit, just to see if I could do it. By the end of the second lap, Anna was still leading the pack in the front, and Marika and the two runners from the back had passed me. In the middle of the third lap, I sped up and tried and tried but couldn't overtake anybody. More than anything, I wanted to stop, but I knew I wouldn't.

I can do it! I can do it! My legs began to move and my arms to pump. *I can do it! I can do it!* My heart beat fast, and I felt strong and in control.

The finish line was close. I forced myself to go even faster and dashed through it dead last before collapsing on the ground.

Ari ran up to me. "You did it!"

The other runners surrounded me. Anna slapped my back.

"Practice is tomorrow afternoon, right after school," Ari said. "I expect to see you there, Jutka!"

32

Sunday, June 9, 1946

*T*he day we had trained for finally arrived. The sports field was abuzz with people. They'd come from other DP camps and also from Austrian civilian teams. My track team was running against a club from town: victory over them would be sweet. Whenever any of us went into Landsberg, we were bombarded with insults. More than anything, we wanted to beat them.

A year ago, we were the walking dead. Today, we were athletes. High jumpers hopped, skipped, and threw themselves into the air at one end of the field while shot-putters grunted and sprung from crouches at the opposite end. Two men were removing hurdles from the track and stacking them up in the field beyond the low metal rail that ran around the inside of the track. Spectators in the bleachers held up banners, yelled, whistled, and stomped. My own team was near the starting line and I hurried to meet them.

Anna ran up to me.

"Where have you been? I was worried that you'd be late!"

"I didn't want to get here too early. I get nervous."

Both Anna and I were running the 1,500. We had practiced hard. She was the fastest runner on the team. I had improved, but I knew that I had no chance of winning. We were dressed in shorts and white T-shirts with Landsberg DP camp written on the back. I kicked off my shoes. The only track shoes Ari had been able to find for me were tight on my feet, so I ran barefoot.

Before the race, Ari gathered us. "I want to tell all of you how proud I am of your hard work. Now, I have a few words for the runners in the 1,500.

"The secret is to concentrate on your pace. You know that you can run this race. You've run it in practice, so you know how fast you can go. You know what you have to do."

He stopped talking suddenly. All of us turned around. A beefy man in a striped jersey was striding toward us, followed by four girls dressed in shiny blue sport shirts, shiny navy shorts, and expensive track shoes. The tallest of them was the blond girl the waiter at the Drei Husaren restaurant had called Fräulein Schiller during Miri's wedding supper. I could tell she recognized me.

Anna stepped forward with her hand extended.

"Hello, I'm Anna . . ."

Her words trailed off as Schiller turned her back.

"What did I say?"

"Nothing," I said. "She is a Nazi!"

The starter announced our event. We moved to the starting line.

The starter raised his pistol. The sound of the shot deafened me, but then I was on my way. As I fought against the other competitors for the inside lane, a sharp elbow jabbed into my side and somebody stomped on my right foot. It was Schiller.

"Prepare to be crushed!"

I didn't reply but focused all of my energy on getting to the inside lane. Schiller was faster than me and beat me to it. As we finished the first lap, Schiller was running beside me in lane one, I was in lane two, and Anna was in lane three next to me. The rest of the runners were in single file behind us.

I tried to remember everything Ari had taught me. I sped up, intending to pass Schiller, but both the Austrian and Anna picked up the pace. My legs began to feel heavy, and my shoulders and chest began to throb. My foot, where Schiller had trod upon it, hurt so badly that it was difficult to run at a steady clip. From the corner of my eye, I saw Anna stumble and fall behind. A stocky girl from the Landsberg team took her place.

By the time we finished the second lap, I felt more confident and decided to speed up again. So did Schiller. The stocky girl on my right moved into my lane, right in front of me, slowing me down.

I have to pass them! I have to pass them! I couldn't do it. When I sped up to sneak between Schiller and her teammate, so did they. When I slowed down, so did they. We completed the third lap with Schiller leading in lane one and the stocky girl a few meters ahead of me in lane two. The runners at the back were far behind the three of us.

The bell rang, signifying the last lap of the race. As I ran by, I saw Ari standing by the side of the track, a stopwatch in his hand, looking furious. I had to do something and had to do it fast. I moved into lane three to pass the two Landsberg runners. The stocky girl also moved into lane three in front of me and Schiller took her place in lane two, still ahead of me. I knew then what I had to do. There was no other way. I swung wide, moved into lane four, and increased my speed. As I headed down the back straightaway toward the curve of the track, all the pain I was experiencing disappeared, and for a few seconds I felt free, as if I were flying. I couldn't see the stocky girl, but Schiller was still ahead of me in lane two.

I tried to speed up even more, but the pain came back, worse than before, slowing me down. My chest hurt, my arms and legs were cramping. The distance between Schiller and me grew even greater.

I was in such agony that I slowed down to stop, but suddenly, the track and the other runners disappeared. There was a train with a long row of cattle cars ahead of me. I was part of a group of Jews running toward it. All of us wore striped uniforms and were barefoot. ss men were lined up in front of the station house in a single file. Their rifles were pointed at us. I knew that I had to run faster than I had ever run before if I wanted to stay alive. I ran and ran until I could not run any longer and fell to the ground panting, trying to catch my breath. I covered my face with my hands to protect myself against the inevitable gunshot.

Ari pried my hands away from my eyes. It took me a second to recognize his face and to remember where I was. He was jubilant.

"You ran a five-minute, thirty-second race!" he cried. "Your last lap was 79.9 seconds – the fastest you've ever run! You beat the Austrian by six full seconds!"

"I won?"

He hugged me.

"You're a champion!"

33

Friday, July 19, 1946

It was a perfect summer day. I lay on my bunk, trying to stay awake, my Hebrew grammar book splayed open on my stomach. I struggled with the letters as long as I could, but the day was too lovely to spend indoors. Sandor was sitting by the door when I came out.

"Is everything all right? Why aren't you at work?" He had been reading the camp newspaper. He rolled it up and put it into his back pocket.

"I'm playing hooky. It's too nice to be cleaning streets. I wanted to ask you to go for a walk. You had the same idea, right?"

The sun warmed our faces as we ambled along, holding hands. We didn't speak much, content with each other's company. I stole a look at Sandor and found his eyes fixed on my face. He looked so handsome, so strong, so decent, with a smile on his lips. We stared at each other for a long moment before bursting into laughter.

"We're so lucky to have found each other," Sandor said. He traced the line of my jaw with a gentle finger. "We'll never be alone again."

I burrowed my head into his neck and held him as tightly as I could.

"How can we be so happy?" I mumbled.

Sandor sighed. He'd heard me ask the same question a thousand times before, and he gave the same reply as he always did. "Our families would want us to be happy."

"Stop it, lovebirds! You're making me jealous!"

I jumped, my cheeks fiery. Margaret was chuckling. She carried a letter.

"It's for you," she said, holding it out. "I hope that it brings you news as good as the letter from Canada."

"What's she talking about?" Sandor asked. "You never told me that you got a letter from Canada."

"Oh . . . It was nothing important. My cousin wrote to me."

"What did she say?"

I forced my voice to sound even. "She offered to help me get my papers to go to Canada. I didn't even reply. I'll write her once we're settled in Eretz Israel."

Sandor looked at me hard.

"Jutka, are you sure that's what you want to do?"

"Of course I'm sure! My mind is made up. I promised, didn't I?"

Margaret cleared her throat. She waved the letter in front of my face. "What about *this* letter? You better take it!"

She pressed it into my hands. I turned it over.

"It's from Hungary, from Julia."

It took all of my willpower to stuff it into the pocket of my skirt without opening it.

"Why are you putting it away?" Sandor asked. "Don't you want to know what she says?"

"I'll read it later."

Margaret must have sensed the tension between us. "I have to leave you now. There is so much to do with all the newcomers."

"What do you mean?" asked Sandor.

"There was a pogrom in Kielce."

"Kielce?" I asked.

"In Poland," she said. "The Jews that survived have had to flee. The first of the refugees are arriving at the camp. My shift on registration is about to start." She hurried off.

"Let's see what's going on," Sandor said, drawing my arm through his.

We came to a sudden stop at the camp gate. A long, restless line of people was being admitted. There were UNRRA and Joint representatives everywhere. The newcomers carried bundles on their shoulders and battered suitcases in their hands. Some of the women held babies in their arms.

Children clung to their parents' hands. Almost all of them were young and strong. They were survivors. A bearded young man with a little boy sitting on his shoulders was doing a little two-step to keep the child amused. Sandor caught his eye. "Welcome," he said in Yiddish.

"Thank you, sir," the man replied. "It's good to be here . . . to feel safe again."

"Are all of you from Poland?"

"Yes." The man dipped the child, making him whoop with delight. "Apparently our suffering in the camps wasn't enough for them," he said sadly. "They killed people in cold blood. Even the police and the army took part in it. We should never have gone back when the war ended."

"That's tragic." Sandor turned to me. "You see, Eretz Israel is the only place for us."

"You're right!" The man yanked his little son's leg gently. "We're going to Eretz Israel, aren't we, buddy?"

"How did you get here?" asked Sandor.

"The Bricha got us out. It was terribly difficult, but here we are."

He reached the front of the line and turned to us to say good-bye.

"Next year in Jerusalem," he smiled.

Sandor walked me back to my block. Neither one of us mentioned the letter from Hungary. It was as if it had never come. He kissed me good-bye and left. I waited until he turned the corner before rushing up the steps two at a time.

I sat down on the edge of the bunk. My hand was trembling so badly that I had difficulty tearing the envelope open. It was stuffed with pages filled with Julia's spidery handwriting.

Pápa, Hungary
May 15, 1946

My dear Miss Jutka,

I was so happy to hear that you survived the war and are well. The mail is very slow. I only received your letter this morning. I hope that my reply will get to you a little faster.

I was so sorry to hear that your mother and grandmother lost their lives. They were wonderful ladies. My heart is broken when I think of the passing of my darling Mrs. Grazer. She was always so kind to me.

I am full of sorrow at the news I must impart to you. Neither your dear papa nor your brother returned home. I heard the same rumors that you must have heard, that both of them were shot while they were serving with their forced labor regiment. I am so sorry for your loss.

The tears in my eyes blinded me. There is knowing something with your head and knowing it with your heart. My heart actually hurt. I wiped away my tears with the back of my hand and continued reading.

It's only my memories that keep me going. Many of those dearest to me in the world are gone. My dear husband passed away last winter. He wasn't the only one. Did you know Miss Szabo? She was a teacher at the gimnazium. I worked for her after I was forbidden from working for Miss Agi's mother any longer. Poor Miss Szabo! She, too, is gone. The Nazis accused her of helping Jewish families escape the authorities. She was executed more than a year ago. I miss my ladies so much.

Now, let me conclude with some good news. My dear Miss Agi came home after the war, in September of last year.

I dropped the letter. Agi is alive! Agi is alive! She must have returned home after Miri left Hungary. I picked up the pages and began to read them again.

She is sadly changed. She walks with a cane and has a terrible limp. I don't know what happened to her, for I didn't think that it was my place to ask. I returned Mrs. Grazer's fur coat to her and her beautiful candlesticks. I hope that you don't mind that I also gave her that book you asked me to keep for you. Miss Agi's young man, Jonah Goldberg, also returned home. He and Miss Agi got married.

I am ashamed to tell you, Miss Jutka, that the Jews who have come back have not been welcomed. People are reluctant to return their belongings. Mr. Jonah changed his name from Goldberg to Gal because it sounds more Hungarian, but it didn't help. He and Miss Agi saw the lay of the land, and they left for Canada. Unfortunately, I don't have their address there. If you find them, please let me know how they're doing. I'd like to write to them.

My dear Miss Jutka, I wish that I had better news for you about your father and brother. Life is so hard nowadays. Please write to me again.

Respectfully yours,

Julia Veres

I folded the letter carefully and put it back into its envelope. My head was throbbing. My papa and brother were really gone. And poor, brave Miss Szabo! I would never forget how she tried to help us. I thought about Agi in Canada and how much I longed to see her. Canada was a big country, but I knew I would be able to find her somehow. And it was where my cousin lived, the only person in the whole world really connected to me.

But I realized that I would never see Agi again or meet my cousin in person. I would never see the Arctic snow, or the mountains or the Indian chiefs in colorful headdresses or the Mounties on horseback in scarlet uniforms. I told myself not to be silly. I loved Sandor and Eretz Israel needed me. A promise is a promise, never to be broken.

34

Friday, August 9, 1946

Once again I was dreaming of Canada.

"Wake up! Wake up!" Somebody was shaking my shoulders. I sat up and rubbed my eyes. Sandor was standing by my bed, his face dappled by the moonlight streaming through the window high up on the wall.

"What's going on? Why are you here?"

"Shhh," he said. "You don't want to wake everybody up!"

The dormitory was dark. The only sound was gentle snoring. He sat down on the edge of my bed.

"A Bricha truck is here, and there is room for us on it!" he whispered into my ear. "It'll take us to the mountains. We'll have to cross the Alps on foot. Then the Bricha will transport us to Milan, where there's a ship heading to Eretz Israel!"

He pulled me up from my bed and hugged me.

"The time's come," he said. "We're finally going home!"

"Do Miri and Natan know?"

"We'll soon find out," he said. "Get dressed as fast as you can. And bring your jacket. It's going to be cold in the mountains at night. I'll pack your knapsack for you."

I threw on the clothes I had worn on the train to Vienna. The moon lit our way to the warehouse at the edge of the camp. Sandor rapped on the door three times. An eye appeared at the peephole, there was the sound of a key being turned, and the doors slid open. Ari motioned for us to enter.

It took a few moments for my eyes to become accustomed to the darkness. At least three dozen men and women and a handful of children were stretched out on blankets. Some were sleeping, but most of them were talking in soft voices. A figure melted out of the shadows and wrapped me in warm arms. It was Miri. Natan followed her.

I patted her stomach.

"I was hoping that you would be here," I said. "How do you feel?"

"Fine," she said. "Tired but fine. I am so happy that Ari made room for us on this transport." Her face softened. "I want my baby to be born in Eretz Israel."

Ari clapped his hands twice. We crowded around him. He gave each of us a loaf of bread and an envelope of forged work permits stating that we were Greek laborers who were allowed to work in the French zone.

"You might need these. We're going to be moving out of

the American sector. We're going to the Alps," he said. "We'll cross the mountains on foot via the Brenner Pass to Italy. A truck will be waiting on the other side to take you to Milan. Your next stop after that will be the coast to board a ship to Eretz Israel."

Ari held up his hand.

"One more thing," he said. "If the authorities stop us, I'll tell them that you are Greek laborers and we're going to Gnadenwald, at the foot of the Alps. If they ask you questions, answer them in Hebrew. They can't tell the difference between Hebrew and Greek."

Within minutes, we had all piled into the back of a canvas-covered truck. Ari got into the driver's seat. Sandor and I were the last ones. I looked out at the dark road behind us. A child was whimpering softly in his mother's lap. Sandor's arm stole around my waist. I leaned my head on his shoulder. Sandor leaned close to my ear.

"What did Julia write to you?" he asked.

"Nothing I wasn't expecting. Papa and Dezso are gone."

"My poor Jutka," Sandor said, pulling me closer. "Did she have any other news?"

"Agi returned home."

"That's great!" Sandor cried. "We'll contact the Bricha to get her out!"

"We can't. She and Jonah got married. They're in Canada somewhere. I am so glad for her. It's what she dreamed of."

"It was your dream too, Jutka," said Sandor pensively.

235

I could see him peering at me through the dark. I turned my head away so that he wouldn't be able to read my expression. He fell silent.

Suddenly, the lights of a car shone through the back of the truck, illuminating our terrified faces. A car was gaining on us. As it shot by, I could see the word *Polizei* written on its side. It swerved across the road, blocking the truck's path. Ari screeched to a halt.

I leaned out. Two uniformed policemen got out of the car, with their revolvers drawn. Ari climbed out of the driver's seat, his arms high in the air. The policemen's guns were pointed at his head.

"Halt!" cried a policeman. "Your documents!"

Ari handed him his papers. The policemen lowered their revolvers.

"Who are these people?" asked the younger of the policemen, pointing at our faces peering out of the back of the truck. "There are Jews trying to escape over the mountains!"

"We're honest Greek laborers, sir," said Ari. "We're on our way to Gnadenwald to work on the farms."

The policemen walked up to the back of our truck. Ari followed them. The older of the officers shone his flashlight into the interior. The light was so bright that I had to shield my eyes with my hands. One of the children began to cry.

"As you can see, officer, we're not bloody Jews!" said Ari. "We're hardworking Greek patriots who have to put food on the table for our families." He turned to Sandor. "Say something to them," he said in Hebrew.

"Get these idiots away from here." Sandor's Hebrew was steady.

"You *are* Greek!" said the older policeman, surprised.

Ari turned toward the cab of the truck.

"Follow me!" he said to the policeman.

"Where do you think you're going?" asked the younger policeman, waving his gun at Ari's head again.

"I want to show you a proof of our good faith, sir," said Ari.

He took two cartons of cigarettes out of the truck and presented one to each policeman.

The policemen stared at each other for a long moment. The older one nodded his head almost imperceptibly. The younger one lowered his revolver.

"It's nice to meet such hardworking Greek people." The younger one snickered.

"On your way!"

Ari jumped into the truck, backed it up, and edged past the police car. The policemen disappeared into the darkness behind us.

We must have traveled another half hour with the Alps looming ahead as our guidepost. Suddenly, we came to a stop. Ari appeared and lowered the back gate of the truck.

"We've reached the mountains," he announced. "Time to get out!"

*

It was completely dark. At first, we followed a path, and it was an easy climb. When we reached a higher altitude, it became colder. Our way was lit by the moon's reflection on the snowy ground. The chill reminded me of the pure white spaces of Canada as I saw them in my dream. As we skirted deep ravines, mothers held on tightly to their children's hands. Several times the trail ended, and we had to pick our way among the trees. I felt lost and disoriented and thankful that Ari knew the way. He'd traveled the same route many times before. The rough scrub under foot made every step treacherous. Miri tripped and fell. She sat down hard on the snowy ground, her leg twisted awkwardly beneath her. Natan tried to pull her up, but as soon as she put weight on her foot she fell back with a groan. Natan cradled her, crooning softly. The others came to a halt. An older man made his way to Miri.

"I am a physician," he said. "Let me take a look at your ankle, my dear."

Miri bit her lip as Natan gently eased off her shoe. The doctor examined her foot with a gentle hand.

"I don't think that it's broken, but you do have a bad sprain. It should be bound, but we don't have bandages."

I tore my knapsack open and took out Frau Schmidt's dress.

"Here, Doctor!"

The physician tugged the material.

"Good and strong," he said. "Perfect for our purposes."

Sandor took out his penknife and cut long strips out of the dress. The doctor wound the cloth around Miri's ankle tightly. Natan helped Miri up. When she tried to put weight on her foot, she moaned and sat down in the snow once again.

"Don't worry, my love," Natan said. "We'll wait here. When the others reach Italy, they'll send us help."

"I am not leaving you!" I crouched down beside her.

"Come on," said Sandor.

He put Miri's arm around his neck and motioned to Natan to do the same.

"We'll be your crutches," he said.

For the rest of the climb, the men took turns supporting Miri as she hobbled over the Alps on one foot.

We arrived on the Italian side of the mountains at daybreak. The rising sun cast a golden glow over our tired faces. Another canvas-covered truck was waiting for us, the driver slouched against its side, a cigarette in his mouth.

"Well, it's time for me to bid you good-bye," said Ari. "I am going back to Landsberg. Sam will take over from here." He nodded to the truck driver. "Good luck to you all!"

We crowded around him, full of gratitude. The women kissed him, the men pumped his hands. We made him promise, over and over again, that he would visit us when he returned to Eretz Israel.

Sam announced that it was time to board. Sandor hopped into the back of the truck. Then he leaned out to help me up. I was about to grab his hand but then hesitated.

I stared at him mutely – my head suddenly full of dreams of sleighs gliding over white snow. I thought of Mama and Papa and how much they loved me. I thought of my grandmother and my brother and how happy they wanted me to be. I thought of Agi and the plans we had made. How much I wanted to find her! I thought of my cousin, my only living relative, waiting for me in Canada. I thought of my dreams that would disappear. But they didn't have to.

"I must talk to you."

Sandor jumped down. "What's the matter?"

I took his hand and led him to the side of the path.

"I've been doing a lot of thinking. I'm not going with you. You're finally beginning to live your dreams. I want to have the same opportunity. Eretz Israel is your dream. Mine is Canada. I'm going back to Landsberg with Ari. My cousin will help me get to Canada."

He grabbed my arm. "Don't be ridiculous! You want to go to Eretz Israel! You promised! I don't want to leave without you!"

I had no more words to say.

"It's time," said the driver.

"Good-bye, my love!" I hugged him tight.

He kissed me hard on the lips and jumped into the back of the truck.

"Ari, Jutka is going back to Landsberg with you," he said. "Take good care of her!"

He disappeared into the truck.

The motor revved. Miri and Natan leaned out and waved

to me, but there was no sign of Sandor. In a few minutes, the truck became a small dot in the Italian landscape.

"It's time to go back," Ari said.

I wiped away my tears.

Glossary

Arrow Cross: Hungarian fascist organization that controlled the government from October 1944 to April 1945 during the Second World War

Ben Gurion, David: the first prime minister of the State of Israel

Bricha (*translation, escape*): illegal immigrant movement of Jews after the Second World War across the occupied zones to the coasts and then by clandestine ships to Eretz Israel. An estimated 80,000 to 250,000 Jews reached Eretz Israel with the Bricha.

cholent: a traditional Jewish Shabbos dish made with meat, beans, and other vegetables and allowed to cook overnight

concentration camp: detention centers set up by Nazi Germany before and during the Second World War for those considered undesirable by the Nazi regime. The prisoners, who included millions of Jews, homosexuals, Jehovah's Witnesses, gypsies, and political prisoners, were terribly mistreated and used for forced labor. Some concentration camps were built to exterminate people; many of the inmates were gassed and their bodies cremated. Auschwitz-Birkenau was the most notorious of these camps.

Displaced Persons (DP) camp: temporary shelter for people who have been left homeless or been forced to flee their home country because of war, persecution, etc.

Eretz Israel: the Land of Israel as it appears in the Bible. It is considered by the Jewish people as their homeland. During the British mandate from 1920 to 1948, this region was officially known both as Palestine and Eretz Israel when written in Hebrew.

gendarme: a type of police officer in Hungary until the end of the Second World War. They were easily identified by their plumed hats.

gimnazium: a Hungarian school with grades five to twelve that provided courses required for university entry

Hagana: the major Jewish underground defense organization of Palestine. After the state of Israel was formed in 1948, the Hagana became the Israeli defense forces.

"Hatikva" (*translation,* "The Hope"): Israel's national anthem

"Hava Nagila": a traditional Jewish song

Hitler, Adolf: the leader of Germany during the Second World War

huppah: Jewish marriage canopy

Jewish Brigade: the only all-Jewish fighting unit that served in the Second World War. It was a part of the British Army. Members of the Jewish Brigade consisted of volunteers from Eretz Israel.

Kodaly, Zoltan: a famous Hungarian composer

kosher: food prepared according to Jewish dietary laws

lecso: Hungarian dish made with rice, peppers, and onions

Mengele, Dr. Josef: a notorious German SS officer and physician in Auschwitz-Birkenau who supervised the selection of arriving Jewish transports and decided who would live and who would be sent immediately to the gas chambers. He performed horrific experiments on camp inmates.

Purim: a joyous Jewish holiday commemorating the time when Jewish people living in Persia were saved from extermination. The story is told in the Bible in the Megillah, the Book of Esther, that's read every Purim.

Rosh Hashanah: Jewish New Year

shaliach (*plural*, shlichim): emissary sent to postwar Europe from Palestine to bring the Jewish survivors to Eretz Israel
Shema: a Jewish declaration of faith used as an important prayer
shul: synagogue, a Jewish house of worship
Star of David: six-pointed Jewish star

Yom Kippur: a sacred Jewish holy Day of Atonement marked by fasting and prayers of repentance; falls eight days after Rosh Hashanah

Pronunciation Guide

Note: In Hungarian, the emphasis is placed on the first syllable of the word. Also, j=y, s=sh, and sz=s.

Agi – Aḡi
Deszo – Dedju
Gyor – Gyūr
Istvan Kicsi – Ishtvan Kichī
Janos – Yanos
Jolan – Yolan
Jutka – Yutka
Lajos – Layos
Sandor – Shandor
Sari – Shari
Szabo – Sabo
Szucs – Sooch

Acknowledgments

I based most of the events in this book upon the experiences of my beloved father and my dear mother in Hungary before the war, in Auschwitz during the Holocaust, and in DP camps after the war ended.

I want to express my deepest gratitude to the four brave souls who also shared their stories with me: Saul (Joil) Alpern, Frank Weinfeld, Morris Faintuch, and Johnny Berkowitz.

I want to express my appreciation for the help given to me by Gisela Persaud, Arie Lavy, Blair DuGray, Jamie Kagan, and Dr. Pamela Orr.

I want to thank my editors Kathy Lowinger and Heather Sangster for never steering me wrong.

Last, but certainly not least, I want to thank my husband and my family for their belief in me, and their encouragement and support.